Death of a Starship

Death of a Starship

Jay Lake

Death of a Starship
Copyright © 2009 Joseph E. Lake, Jr.

Cover illustration © 2009 Tony Shasteen

A MonkeyBrain Books Publication
www.monkeybrainbooks.com

No part of this book may be reproduced or transmitted in any form or by any means, graphic, electronic, or mechanical, including photocopying, recording, taping, or by any information storage or retrieval system, without the permission in writing from the publisher.

MonkeyBrain Books
11204 Crossland Drive
Austin, TX 78726
info@monkeybrainbooks.com

ISBN: 1-932265-29-5
ISBN: 978-1-932265-29-3

Printed in the United States of America
10 9 8 7 6 5 4 3 2 1

Second battle of 3-Freewall, more than a baseline century past

"Z-flotilla's gone over to the rebels!" shouted one of the comm ensigns. Sweat beaded on the boy's shaved scalp. He was still young enough to be excited by combat.

NSS *Enver Hoxha*'s battle bridge was wedge-shaped, command stations at the narrow aft end, a giant array of displays at the blunt forward end, everything finished out in military-grade carbonmesh and low-intensity gel interfaces. A dozen duty stations were arrayed before and below Captain Saenz, eighteen officers and enlisted laboring wet-backed and trembling in the service of their own imminent death. Everything reeked of panicked men and distressed electronics.

Commander Ulyanov leaned close, his bullet head gleaming sweat bright as the ensign's. "They're not firing... yet. With respect sir, we're done. All the other capital assets have gone over or been neutralized."

"Neutralized" in deep space meant decompressive death for hundreds or thousands of crew, the survivors scattering like sparks from a bonfire in lifepods that were more likely to be used as ranging targets than ever be rescued within their survival windows. Except in a civil war, when it could also mean officers lined up in boat bays and gunned down by excited sailors acting under mutinous orders.

Captain Saenz stared at the main displays, all shunted to internal status reports. Everything glowed amber or red. The battle bridge shuddered, gravimetrics cycling on a decay curve tending asymptotically toward catastrophic failure. He'd had damage control shut down the alarms, even the strobes. Too many of the *Hoxha*'s systems were critical or supercritical. If any of the new skippers in Z-flotilla worked up the nerve to open fire on their erstwhile heaviest asset, those systems wouldn't matter to anyone but an after-action forensics team. Imminent death had become remarkably quiet. "I will *not* strike my colors," he muttered.

"Then they'll strike 'em for us, Rod."

"So we withdraw."

Ulyanov glanced around the bridge. Saenz wondered if his first officer were on the brink of switching loyalties. Was he counting heads? Or sidearms? But no, the exec turned his gaze back to the captain, guile absent from his eyes. "Where to? This is… was… the last Loyalist fleet."

"Anywhere outside this disaster area."

"We've only got one contingent withdrawal course still open. And the window on that beacon's getting more and more narrow."

Saenz chopped a hand down. "Go."

Ulyanov slid a hand over his console, setting off stored actions plans. "Attention on bridge," he said. "We are implementing contingency gamma seven, effective—"

Something hit them hard enough to flop the battle bridge's multiply redundant, hardened gravimetrics. Polarity cycled several times in rapid succession, bouncing everything that wasn't strapped down between the deck and the overhead. Lights dimmed and blowers cut out as the *Hoxha*'s engineering section routed power to the c-drivers.

Larger ships had an inherent advantage in reaching the lightspeed discontinuity, especially deep in stellar gravity wells. Somewhere at the bottom, the equations rested in part on $F_{net} = m*a$, which in turn drove Higgs boson crowding and enabled the c-transition. Larger ships had larger mass, and in c-physics the value of mass in the equation scaled more rapidly than the value of acceleration.

In other words, once *Hoxha* lurched into motion, for all that her tormentors could literally fly rings around her, she'd make her exit from the battle into the ghostly reaches of c-space long before they could follow the negative energy traces of her wake. As long as her systems were sufficiently whole when she reached transition speed, that was.

Captain Saenz watched his light pen find a stable resting point in three pieces on the floor. "Think we should have drunk those last bottles of wine in the executive wardroom, Georgi?"

Ulyanov laughed. "There's always tomorrow. Give us another seven minutes on this acceleration power curve and we'll live to see it."

Four minutes and change later, Z-flotilla decided it had new orders and began pouring firepower into *Hoxha*'s aft ventral armor and shields. Saenz declined to return fire in favor of maintaining shield strength and keeping his ship moving. The battle bridge grew vacuum-quiet, save for the crackling ripple from the gravs. The damage control figures flickered on the main display so fast the human eye couldn't track any more.

"Still going to make it," Ulyanov said. It was more of a question, or perhaps a prayer, than a statement.

Saenz watched the numbers toll the death knell of his

ship. Forward and dorsal shields were down completely. His crew strength was below thirty-five percent effective. Damage control parties under Commander Poolyard were a hundred and forty-two percent committed. Which meant there were fires and worse raging unchecked in *Hoxha*'s belly. "Depends on what else they hit us with."

"Rod...."

Here it comes, thought Saenz. Eyes still on the main screen, his hand drifted to his fléchette pistol. "Too late, Commander. We're too late to do anything else."

"Listen. Please. I—"

Whatever Ulyanov had been about to say was lost in a blare of navigation alarms. "Not now!" screamed Lieutenant Commander Dürer. "We've got a mass moving into our c-transition space!"

Any collision almost certainly meant an extremely violent energy exchange, rendering *Hoxha* into a minor sun for a few moments.

"Drop shields," Saenz ordered. "Drop environmental power. All nonengine power to forward batteries. Vaporize it."

With that, the funereal hush of the bridge imploded, a cascade of shouts in the increasingly stale and smoky air.

"It's about two percent of our mass, captain!"

"Batteries two, three, and seven offline, sir. Six and eight are... they're... gone, sir! Just not there anymore."

"Not a rock, it's altering course."

"Not one of ours... er, theirs. Nothing we know, I mean. No IFF signature, wrong composition."

"It's a fucking self-propelled asteroid!"

"Language, Lieutenant."

"It's absorbing over fourteen terawatt/seconds of firepower, sir. And it's still *there!*"

In the midst of the chaos, Captain Saenz watched the main screen. It now displayed a simplified diagram of *Hoxha*'s escape trajectory. The erratic motions of the interfering mass were plotted in an intersecting curve.

"You have anything to do with this, Georgi?" he asked in a few seconds of random quiet.

"I don't want to die, sir," said Ulyanov. "Not this way or any other."

"No one wants to die, my friend." Saenz found his hand was still on his pistol. "But how many of us get to live forever?"

Then there was more fire pounding the unprotected aft of the ship, and an explosive pressure vent between hull frames 127 and 144, and the mystery mass was still inside their escape trajectory, and the purple c-lights stuttered on as the battle bridge gravs shut down completely and a horrendous, tooth-shattering wrench overtook *Hoxha* and her crew as they disappeared forever into a screaming white light.

#

Menard: Nouvelle Avignon, Prime See

The Grand Ekumenical Basilica towered more than a kilometer into the violet Avignard sky. The edifice was a vast, eye-bending twist of titanium and carbonmesh sheathed with glittering spun diamond glass in every color known to man. Red-winged angel-flyers circled it endlessly, security in the air matched by ground-based, orbital, and virtual assets even more fearsome for being inconspicuous. Diamond windows, angels and all, the building was a giant, shouted prayer to the Lord God, a celebration of the glory of creation and man's place in it. That the Church used that glory to impress the Emperor and his court, not to mention all the pilgrims and tourists, was a collateral benefit to His earthly servants. As if in response from Heaven, lightning played perpetually around the shining crosses that gleamed through every night and were supposedly even visible from orbit.

Not that the Very Reverend Jonah Menard, Chor Episcopos in the ranks of the holy and mid-level functionary of the Church, had ever been able to spot them in his frequent comings and goings.

Once more down the gravity well. As it happened, he had business outside the long, glorious shadow of the tower, down amid the featureless warren of offices in which the majority of the functions of the Church were conducted. He was bound for the Xenic Bureau of the Grand Ekumenical Security Directorate—his own department. Like almost all of the Ekumen Orthodox Church's vast and tentacled bureaucracy, the Xenic Bureau was housed quite sensibly in an underground building out of the public eye. The Bureau's quarters were a multilayered maze of identical concrete corridors and meeting rooms and cubicles, with a perhaps higher than normal concentration of virteolizer rooms—the Xenic Bureau spent a lot of time working inside its collective imagination.

Chor Episcopos Menard was a short man, not at all like the popular image of either a humble parish priest or one of the grand patriarchs of the Church. He was barrel-chested with an unfortunate run toward fat and knees that ached from a lifetime of kneeling too much. His forehead was tattooed with the three-barred Orthodox cross in a deep green ink that matched the shade of his eyes, his scalp dark with razor stubble. Though he could argue doctrine with all the fervor of his University of Romagrad Th.D., Menard was also one of the Church's leading experts on xenic intelligences. Such as they were, and such as they might exist.

And while the Church had one set of complex, nuanced views on this topic, the Empire had quite another.

"Jonah." It was Bishop Antonine Russe, his manager and a reserve commodore in the Church Militant, the Patriarch's fleet. Russe was every centimeter the spare, ascetic churchman of the popular imagination, affecting the black-and-white robes of the highest formal levels of the Patriarchate. Russe shaved his head, and even his eyebrows, and sported an elaborate tattoo across the curve of his scalp. His pectoral cross was meteoric iron, heavy enough that its chain left a raw circle always visible around his neck.

Menard inclined his head. "Sir. I am reporting in."

"Skip the log-ins and pop down to conference room Yellow-2 with me."

The Chor Episcopos suppressed a sigh. "Yes, sir."

"This one's big. Worth the trouble. Trust me, Jonah."

The problem was, Menard didn't trust Russe. Not one bit.

#

Golliwog: Powell Station, Leukine Solar Space
Clutching the flint sparker in the palm of his left vacuum glove, Golliwog flew tight and hard along the curve of the hull. The exercise was being conducted in and around the derelict hull of an old quartermaster's transport bottom—a dead slow pig designed to move enormous amounts of material from one gravity well to another. Dummy or not, it wasn't a simulation. At some point in training, simulations became meaningless. Golliwog could be killed here, yes he could. Even as he brushed a meter or so above the highest hull protrusions, he watched for weaponsign.

The enemy was crafty. Golliwog knew that. He knew the enemy well because the enemy was him.

There... he spotted a flash high on his port flank.

The assault sled's primitive instrumentation began blinking at about the same time. Golliwog flipped over, killed all his power—thrust, instrumentation, comm, everything—and fingered the switches he'd welded onto the panel that morning. They controlled the release valves on eight bottles of high-pressure oxygen welded to the sled frame.

Now he was a ballistic object steered with squirts of O_2. His albedo, including sled and weapons, was about one percent. Still high, but it was the best he could do within the training parameters. Bright as nanotrace fog in direct starlight, the sparkle of the oxygen venting would be a dead giveaway, but he'd stayed in the shadowed side of the monstrous ship so long the enemy had been forced to come looking for him.

Golliwog cleared his mind and set most of his internal systems into rest mode. Dangerous, that, but useful, too. Shutting down both his internals and the sled meant he was just a piece of junk, inert mass that had broken off the training hull. Pay no mind to the kilos of protein: On a training sled the enemy's sensor suite wouldn't be wired to look for that anyway. He hoped. The enemy was, by definition, as clever as he was.

Froggie never believed in giving up advantages. Golliwog's combat mentor would beat him blue and senseless for a trick like this, but Froggie wasn't out here alone in the hard vacuum. Old Anatid, on the other hand, would probably approve of the skewed thinking. Anatid was Golliwog's strategy mentor, an ancient bione with a cryptic manner who'd befriended Golliwog even beyond the confines of the training rooms.

Unpowered, quiet as an empty airlock, he hurtled along the shadowed side of the hull, twisting the flint sparker in his hand for luck, or nerves. Where was that flash again? Golliwog watched the high port flank, stalking the enemy who was stalking him.

Then the other sled was *in front* of him, turning under sudden acceleration in a faint glow of ionized exhaust gas. Golliwog flipped the triggers on his starboard oxygen bottles and rolled along his axis just as his own sled took a solid hit of a directed energy lance. The little instrumentation panel flared bright, then glowed dead, even as the shock caused Golliwog's entire body to spasm. The only thing that saved him was the fact that he was in shutdown mode. Shunts and breakers absorbed the invading currents before they could fry the idle cognitive and reactive systems.

Still alive, thought Golliwog. Old Anatid would be proud. *The enemy believes me fried to a ballistic lump.* He triggered his aft ventral bottle, calculating the pull to vent the escape valve at just the right speed to flip his sled end over end and send it crashing into the enemy's sled stern-first, the relatively heavy propulsion unit slamming into the enemy's fairing.

"Where's your power now!" Golliwog screamed, breaking protocol. He laughed as he hotstarted his combat mods and popped free from his safety clips, one hand on the sled's steering bar so he didn't spin loose. The exercise required him to wear only a skin suit, no combat armor, and he could carry no issue weapons. (*And where had the enemy gotten a DE lance?* asked a traitor voice in his head.) Instead he had another oxygen bottle strapped to his waist, along with a bottle of liquid hydrogen—each of them with a line rigged to one of his gloves.

Where was the enemy?

The enemy solved that problem by presenting himself, leading with a long-handled hook. A deadly weapon in a vacuum fight, that. Golliwog twisted around his own axis with a tiny squirt of oxygen from his left wrist. He grabbed the enemy's hook just behind the blade, then swung his left leg up for a grip. He brought his wrists together pointing at the enemy, opened the valves on both bottles, and clicked the sparker.

In the blooming light of thrust and fire, Golliwog saw the surprise on his own face within the enemy's helmet.

#

Albrecht: Halfsummer, Gryphon Landing
Micah Albrecht had always liked ship models as a child. R-class hunter-seekers, the old pre-Imperial battlewagons, even spin-racing yachts. He'd built them all, filled two rooms until his dad had thrown the ships out, along with him. Which, in a sense, was why he now wandered the too-hot open-air market in Gryphon Landing, too many light-years from anywhere he belonged, angry and desperate.

His fascination with ships and all their doings eventually led him to be a c-drive engineer. Well, he *had* been one, damn it. Albrecht had lost his certification thanks to a witch hunt and a bought-off tribunal on board the *Princess Janivera*. They'd needed somebody to take the blame for the environmental crash that had left three paying passengers brain-dead. The union steward wasn't about to let his nephew go down for it, even though the little bastard was rotten as month-old milk—guilty but uncharged.

Albrecht had been lucky to stay out of prison. Of course, if the whole mess had gotten into criminal court, the fix might have been uncovered, so the owners had generously ensured that charges were not brought.

Now he wandered the cramped alleys between market stalls under a powder-blue sky somebody had told him was a dead ringer for old Earth. How the hell they'd known that was beyond him. The market was chaos, of course, crowded and pulsing as any dock, even if this was the last port of call for most of the people and the things they bought and sold.

The booths ranged from a bit of fabric between two saplings all the way to powered cargo containers with their own internal cooling and feelie shows. The merchandise ran the gamut of everything he could imagine finding for sale in a third-rate port town, with the possible exception of human beings. The whole place reeked of machine oil and the ozone-sharp scent of distressed electronics, with a side of the eel curry that seemed to be the ground state of dirtside food.

When all else was done, eat the damned eels out of the recycling tanks. Last rule of survival on a dying station. Eating eel was one step away from death.

He paused before a gnarled man in a grubby dhoti sitting on a tarp cut from solar sail fabric. Spread out before the old man were an array of oddly shaped tools and parts, most of them with that dull luster of space-rated equipment.

Oh ho, thought Albrecht.

He squatted opposite the old man. Without making eye contact, he scanned the merchandise. These had come from a c-drive ship, Albrecht was certain. There was no mistaking the Higgs sniffer, used for fault tracing in a c-drive secondary transform block. Some of the mechanical tools had wider applications, to be sure—that mil-spec valve corer was out of an environmental maintenance kit.

He picked up a codelock key, mostly from sheer curiosity.

"Three creds," the old man said with a heavy Alfazhi accent.

"Worthless," Albrecht responded automatically. In point of fact, a codelock key was worthless only off its programmed ship. He turned the device over in his hand. Also mil-spec, Naval issue. Though it had the oddly squared look of some previous generation of tech. Most Naval stuff you saw today was streamlined, as if even their coffeemakers had to survive reentry.

Someone had punched out the smartspot on the inventory tag, then ground the ship's name off with a file, though a keel number was still mostly visible. A lot of trouble for a thief to go to, patiently whittling at the metal of something that was essentially three hundred grams of junk. "See," he said, "no ship for it."

The old man grinned and waved his hand. "You buy else more, I give you. Nice paperweight for busy man, ah?"

Albrecht needed a paperweight about as much as he needed a waterlung, but he smiled anyway. He sorted through the rest of the gear. Albrecht knew to the decicredit what the portside pawnshops paid for usable ship's tools. He couldn't take the valve corer—pawning mil-spec was illegal. Some of the other stuff was fine. The inertial torsion wrenches were generic, no inventory tags. The Higgs sniffer would be nice, if it worked, but it was tagged. Too easy to trace.

He touched the three wrenches and a pair of ion coupling spacers. "Five credits all." They'd be worth fifteen, two, maybe fifteen, five over at Honest Al-Qadi's. If he could clear five on the deal, that was tonight's mattress fee paid.

"Twelve," the old man said through another smile.

He only had ten on him to start with... his day's seed money, tugged from a diminishing stash carefully hidden away in a portside wall. Albrecht held out, and they settled at eight, five. Taking his seed money back out, that left him mattress money and enough to buy a bowl and twenty minutes of seating in front of the stewpot at the Crewman's Rest that afternoon.

Eel stew. *Every day's just another day*, he told himself, walking away in his perpetual slump.

"Hey, sailor!" shouted the old man.

Albrecht turned and to his surprise caught the code key out of the air.

"For your papers, ah!" The old bastard laughed. Albrecht just nodded, then continued walking.

#

Menard: Nouvelle Avignon, Prime See

Conference room Yellow-2 hosted a colloquium of Xenic Bureau division heads. Nothing was more boring than a division executive meeting as far as Menard was concerned. At least, not usually. They were in the dark, a big virteo screen running a rapid series of graphics. It smelled like a meeting, too many people with onions for lunch and the faint sweat of boredom.

Oh God, Menard prayed, *grant me the strength to suffer whatever this is that Your servant and my master has put me up to*. He was immediately ashamed at praying for such trivia, but not ashamed enough to express contrition.

Sister Pelias was talking. She was the lone woman in the entire Bureau, division head of Systems Trend Analysis, which mostly did pattern matching on equity market trades and communications routing. Chor Episcopos Menard privately thought she was a compelling argument against the sheer idiocy of barring women from the hierarchy. It wasn't his job to comment on that.

"Chor Episcopos Menard," she said, her light pen bobbing as she nodded at him. "I was just discussing the Kenilworth–Marsden hypothesis. If one is willing to take K-M analyses at face value, they would indicate a strong possibility of xenic influence in the Front Royal sector. This is based on the, well, *bending*, of comm routing primarily. We've also seen some out-of-norm fluctuation in the futures markets traded in Front Royal and several neighboring sectors, again mapping into K-M.

"Now, in and of itself, these aren't terribly significant. I can pull positive K-M events out of any corner of the empire within any annualized data set. But...." She paused to switch viewing modes on the display. "If we track public health reporting across Front Royal, we can correlate incidents of schizophrenia, paranoia and... well... please excuse me, Bishop, religious mania. This is, of course, the classic Whitley hypothesis. Much like K-M curves, I can build a Whitley curve in any number of places."

The images on the virteo flickered again, the two curves overlaying with a potentially meaningful degree of fidelity. Menard found himself interested despite his skepticism about the meeting.

Sister Pelias continued. "What is significant is how these two map together. We're seeing at least five other indicators trending on similar curves. In other words, gentlemen, the ghosts we've been tracking in our machines all these years are lining up. I can't tell you what it means. Quite probably it signifies nothing whatsoever, but we must attend to the possibility."

Bishop Russe cleared his throat. "Thank you, Sister Pelias." His dry tones managed to make her name into something insulting. "Chor Episcopos Menard has finally arranged to join us." Jonah winced at that. "Perhaps Father Bainbridge would care to enlighten the Very Reverend Jonah as to what his Signals Analysis team has uncovered."

It went on for several hours like that, elusive clues and strange possibilities that almost made sense when you tried to match them up. Nothing as strong as Sister Pelias's data, tenuous as even that was. Nonetheless, Menard was itching to talk privately to her, while the Bishop continued to drag them through the whole formal protocol of the meeting. That suggested something important was up, something that Russe wanted to have his backside covered for in the Bureau's records. This whole lights-and-orbit show was for the future report-reading benefit of someone higher up in the Grand Ekumenical Security Directorate.

When the meeting finally broke up, Menard managed to duck Russe and follow Sister Pelias out into the hallway. "Magda," he said, catching up to her.

"Jonah," she said. "Nice to see you again."

Sister Pelias was a slim woman worn through by time. Menard had never seen her without her wimple, so he had no idea about her hair, but her eyebrows were a pale gold shot with silver. She wore no tattoo at all, unusual for someone with any seniority in the hierarchy. But then, a woman anywhere in the hierarchy outside the female orders was unusual.

"What do you really think," he asked as they walked along, air dampers clicking and thumping above them, pumping out a vaguely moldy breeze. "About your section's findings?"

"I think I could correlate the price of eggs in the local marketplace with the surface temperatures on Jojoba if I wished to. Do these data sets mean anything?" She shrugged, a sort of odd movement as she walked. "I don't know. It is our job to look for significance, and so we see significance. Whether what we discover corresponds to reality, well, that is someone else's problem."

"My problem, I'm afraid," said Menard.

"Well, yes. Pareidolia is wired deep into human perception. We see what we want to see, everywhere we look." She walked for a moment in silence, her low heels sliding against the floor. "Jonah...."

This was what he was waiting for. She knew something. "Whatever it is," he said softly, "I would very much like to hear it."

"I'm... you know I'm not an Externalist."

"Right." Menard found Externalism laughably improbable. It was wish fulfillment from people who looked beyond the margins of the Empire for something better. As if xenics haunted human space in untraceable ships, ever on the verge of revealing miracles and wonders if only poor man proved himself worthy. A poor substitute for God's hand in creation. Unfortunately, about a third of Bishop Russe's division heads were Externalists. Including, perhaps, Russe himself.

"Even so, something's up. Something's moving out there."

"By the pricking of your thumbs?"

She gave him a sharp-eyed look. "By the pricking of my data, more like it. But no, if you must know, by the pricking of Bishop Russe's thumbs. I'm reasoning from effect, not cause, in this case. There's too much interest flowing down from the upper reaches of the Security Directorate. For years, we've been a joke, a line item in the budget. The rest of the Church sees this Bureau as a collection of nutcases serving as some kind of lowball insurance policy against any of this being real. The last couple of months you've been gone, we've become, well... important."

"What do you believe, Sister?" Menard trusted this woman's intuition.

"I don't often admit to what I'm about to say, but I believe you need to consider it. If I have a position, I suppose you'd say I was an Internalist. It doesn't affect my work, I have come to that position from a perspective of intellectual consistency more than anything. Nonetheless, here I am, wondering if that thought exercise of mine has the ring of truth somewhere inside it."

That was a fascinating position for someone as hardheaded as Sister Pelias. "Internalism is difficult to demonstrate logically. How do you explain the supposed presence of xenics in the halls of government and commerce?"

"No explanation. Insufficient data, and too much speculation in the literature."

"I…don't take either position, Sister. As you probably know." Menard's specialty was physical evidence of xenic presence. Of which there was remarkably little, and none of that incontrovertible. In practice, that meant he spent a lot of time looking at oddly shaped asteroids or wandering through overgrown jungle sites. He'd made a sideline in profiling xenic methods and motives. It was something to do during the long periods of travel. "But you believe something's up."

"I believe something's up."

After all the centuries, was it possible? Was the human race finally about to meet someone else? Angels might well have once walked the earth, in Biblical times, but *Homo sapiens* had been alone in space since Gagarin first went to Mars.

The thought chilled Menard's bones, a mixture of thrill and fear. Maybe it was real. He thanked God that this possibility had come in his lifetime, and prayed that he might have a role.

#

Bishop Russe walked into Menard's office as Menard was checking the timestamps and action receipts on his filings. Menard had sent his mission report in from system transit, as soon as the Church courier he'd hitched a ride with had dropped in from c-space to decelerate toward Nouvelle Avignon.

"What did you find on Ancira?" Russe asked.

Menard sighed. Russe had already receipt-and-acknowledged the reports. "What do I ever find? Enormous stone blocks deep in a jungle more green than death, snakes thicker than your waist. Proof? If I wanted to wish hard enough, I could have convinced myself they'd been carved by xenics."

Russe laughed. "We might be on to a change."

I'll bet, thought Menard. *I was in the same meeting you were in.* "Your Grace?"

A thin, spidery arm slid across Menard's shoulders. "This could make all our reputations. All the way into the Grand Basilica. If we uncover evidence of a threat to the Empire, a threat to the Church, a threat to our very souls, if we expose the serpents that walk freely among us already... we will be heroes, Jonah. Saints someday, perhaps."

Menard didn't particularly want to be a saint. And the Bishop wasn't inspiring his confidence. But this was his moment, a potential tipping point in history. Perhaps God had set Russe's obsessions into motion as a sign to Menard. Though he hated the politics of office and hierarchy, he tried to play the games when they needed to be played. He *had* to secure leave to pursue this. "Indeed, sir?"

"Think, Chor Episcopos. Our own people say the data indicates it's happening in the Front Royal sector. Halfsummer seems likely. The xenics are gathering at Halfsummer, looking for something. Will you go there and lend your expertise?"

Menard almost shivered once more from the chill in his bones. He could feel the prickle of inspiration. "It would be an honor, Your Grace. A calling, perhaps."

Russe smiled. "I knew you could be counted on, Jonah. Go there and find me a xenic."

"Oh, believe me, I shall." *With God as my witness*. Menard knew he suffered from the sin of pride, but sometimes pride was necessary to drive a man to new heights.

#

Golliwog: Powell Station, Leukine Solar Space
Golliwog was strapped in on his back in the question chair in one of the exam rooms, at the bottom of a step-sided funnel. This resulted in his looking up into a rounded, widening space as the examiners leaned over their individual podiums and looked down upon him. A bank of lights at the far end of the room glared too-brightly, while the metal and carbonmesh tiers rising above him looked like something on the verge of collapsing downward.

All in all, a masterpiece of psychological architecture. The view was profoundly disconcerting. As was the persistent rumor that particularly unlucky examinees were dropped out of the bottom of the funnel and into somewhere terminally unpleasant deep within the convoluted bowels of Powell Station.

He looked up at Froggie, Admiral Penrose, and Dr. Yee. Old Anatid wasn't in the room, which worried Golliwog. Old Anatid was the only one who would have approved of his solution. Froggie he trusted, Admiral Penrose was just doing her job, and Dr. Yee was… Dr. Yee. To be avoided whenever possible.

But by vacuum, he'd succeeded. Golliwog smiled. For some reason, the three above him shifted.

"Golliwog," said Froggie in his sternest mentor voice. The teacher was the oldest human Golliwog had ever met, but also one of the strongest. "We are here to score your exercise performance. That score, and the opinions of this Examining Board, will weigh into your next duty detail."

Golliwog's smile slipped away at that statement. Training, training, training. He had been training, yes he had, since he could remember. Once there had been so many of him he couldn't count them all. Then there were fewer, and fewer. He'd first killed himself at the age of seven. Now, well, there was only one of him left. Though Golliwog knew with a cold, sometimes comforting certainty that there were other classes of biones in Powell Station going through the surgeries, the training, the bone-grinding pain—other clutches of same-faced killers committing serial murder–suicide. Others unlike him, striving to reach… something.

"I am ready, sir and ma'ams."

Froggie glanced at Admiral Penrose. The Admiral, who was an apparently unremarkable woman except for her rank, nodded. "GLW 317," she said slowly, "in the matter of the recent exercise, this Board deems that you have passed by right of survival." She leaned a little further over. "This is known informally as the last man standing clause. While some of us may not endorse your methods, the results make their own case." She glanced briefly back at Froggie. "Speaking personally, I found your conduct of the exercise refreshing and even somewhat original. It is the judgment of this Board that you are to be granted a passing grade, without censure or demerit."

Golliwog had never doubted that he had passed. The fact that he was still breathing was proof of that. But they could have bounced him back down the training cycle.

Dr. Yee took up a paper in her hand. She was a tiny woman, skin almost space-black, with huge round eyes. She was also one of the few people who frightened

Golliwog. "It is further the recommendation of this Board that you be released to an operational mission. Your assignment will be on a brevet basis, working under a senior agent of the Office of Naval Oversight. That agent will have complete authority over you as an asset, including the right to order your termination. Do you accept this assignment?"

An assignment. To be free of training after almost two decades. In spite of himself, Golliwog smiled once more. He would finally be out of Powell Station. "Yes, ma'am. I accept."

"You will report to me at 06:00 hours tomorrow. You are free to go."

Froggie shook his head.

The restraints unsnapped. The Examining Board filed out of an exit on their tier. Golliwog sat alone at the bottom of the room, which seemed filled with ghosts and echoes. All of him, at all different ages. He'd reached something they'd all been straining for since before memory began.

He just wasn't sure what it was.

No proctors came for him. After a while, Golliwog pulled himself up out of the chair and stood on the rim of the lowest level of the exam room.

Free to go where, Golliwog wondered. He'd never been free to do anything.

#

Golliwog sat in a study carrel in the research library. The room was high-ceilinged, three decks, one of the few decorative spaces he'd ever seen. Most compartments on Powell Station were functional. Sometimes that function was behind the eyes of the beholder. He thought that might be the case here, but Golliwog didn't have many semiotic associations for the idea of "library." It was just a quiet place, trimmed with wood pillars and long falls of fabric, featuring many terminals and a few hardbooks. And sometimes people who helped you learn to ask better questions of the systems.

He wasn't here studying anything, he just didn't know where else to go. His training cadre's suite was shut down for cleaning, so he'd come here. He was looking at a randomly selected virteo about the nut trade on Fentress-IIb when Old Anatid found him.

Golliwog suspected that Anatid was younger than Froggie, but the mentor had been through something somewhere that had fried a lot of his systems, both human-norm biological and bione enhanced. The mentor's skin was puckered with worm-track scars, and he sometimes smelled of ozone. All through Golliwog's life, Old Anatid had disappeared for a few days every month or so for deep medical treatment. The Navy wouldn't waste this much effort on a bione if he wasn't exceptionally valuable, but Old Anatid had a way with the Golliwogs of Powell Station.

Golliwog wasn't certain what else went on at Powell Station, but the training of the bione classes clearly consumed a large amount of attention, resources, and energy. Old Anatid was part of that.

"It's always a test, boy," said Old Anatid, dragging a chair from a nearby carrel.

Golliwog shut off the virteo. "I know."

"What would you do cut off from support on a public station? Or in a dirtside city?"

Golliwog smiled. "Is that a training question?"

"No." Anatid waved vaguely. "No more than everything else is in this life. They could have given you a bunk assignment and a meal chitty. Everyone else on station has one. They're letting you dangle, boy."

"And so I dangle, sir."

Old Anatid watched him for a while. Golliwog

stared back—he was quite good at that. It wasn't the cold-eyed assessment of Dr. Yee, or a surgeon about to replace his long bones. There was something more like fondness, even kinship in that look.

"You'll be briefed… eventually," Anatid finally said. "But if it were me going out right now, I might take some interest in the xenic question."

Golliwog's training had included an excellent education. He could speak six languages, service a c-drive or a gravimetric trap generator, and synthesize poisons from over two hundred Terran-standard plants. He wasn't used to being completely uninformed about something. "The xenic question, sir?"

"You're in a library. Use it. Just know there's been some quiet whispers of concern lately, in certain very high offices." Old Anatid stood up, patted Golliwog on the head, and left.

#

patron17: tell me about xenics

Library: Would you like a definition?

patron17: yes

Library: Xenic, n. and adj., One of or pertaining to nonhuman intelligences rumored to be acting on human affairs and conducting espionage and sabotage within Imperial space.

patron17: are they real

Library: The xenic influence has never been verified. Existence of xenics has never been conclusively demonstrated.

patron17: why do people believe

Library: Many reasons. These reasons include cultural paranoia, caution in the face of a hostile environment, and the apparent human need for an external enemy. There are also chains of circumstantial evidence which can be accounted for by assuming xenic influence.

patron17: what is the xenic question

Library: In its simplest form, the xenic question asks whether xenic intelligences exist.

patron17: tell me about the more complicated forms of the xenic question

Library: A librarian will assist you shortly. Please remain where you are.

#

Albrecht: Halfsummer, Gryphon Landing

Men were stacked in the godown like inventory, spread out on shelving that ran six layers high, originally configured for something about half a meter tall and slightly longer than the average male human being. Albrecht had scored an upper bunk, not trapped beneath four or five layers of sweating, snoring, muttering indigents, with the odd bedwetter thrown in for variety. Five credits was a lot for a mattress fee, but it bought him a day cycle's worth of residency permit. Gryphon Landing wasn't kind to the truly homeless.

At least he knew something about ship parts and tools. It was a living, more or less. Albrecht had no idea how many of the mass of torpid men around him scored their five creds a day. From the dreamtime moaning that went on all night, he didn't want to know.

It was hot, of course. Everything was hot on Halfsummer. And the godown had no climate control, just vent fans high up in the rafters among the flittermice and the feral cats. The lucky ones around him snored their way through the eye-watering fug, but a lot of nights, like this one, Albrecht found the stench overwhelming. Every time he opened his mouth to breathe, he felt like he was drowning in sweat, spit, blood, jizz.

At least he had air above him. If the top bunks were purgatory, the lower bunks were hell. All of them were here for their sins, of course. Planetary citizens had other places to go. Women had other places to go. His neighbors were men who'd tumbled down the gravity well one too many times, without a ticket back up, without the right money or certifications or skills or state of sobriety to climb Jacob's ladder back to the spare, environmentally conditioned heaven of a berth on a ship heading outsystem.

He wasn't like them, Albrecht told himself. He was a better man, a smarter man, just down on his luck. What kept him awake, even more than the salty, sweaty reek that enveloped him like a mother's love, was the thought that everyone in this place believed the same thing about himself.

#

Morning found Albrecht on the street again, all his worldly goods in a thigh pack strapped to the leg of his shipsuit like always. The stupid codelock key hadn't fit, so he was carrying it around in his hand. It had occurred to him to wonder if the Public Safety patrols might interpret it as weapon, sort of a fistpack or sap.

He decided he didn't care. It was a bright, sunny day, with those strange, flat Halfsummer clouds in the sky. Gryphon Landing was as low and crumpled as ever, skyline marred by half-built buildings marooned in the last equity crash, lined with peculiar puffy-leaved trees that smelt like old tea bags.

Something rumbled overhead, staggering through the peak overpressure point of the local speed of sound. Albrecht didn't bother to look up anymore—nothing flew that wanted his sorry butt on board. Instead he turned the codelock key over in his hand.

Why would someone file off the ship name but not the keel number? That was fairly pointless. Anyone with nöosphere access could research the keel easily enough.

What the hell, he thought. It was free day at the library. He could go research the keel number himself. Maybe this had been on a ship he'd built a model of once. The damned steward had dropped his models in the mass converter on the *Princess Janivera*, along with everything else Albrecht couldn't carry away in two hands. At any rate, that gave him something to do in the hours before the market got into full swing once more. Spacers weren't early morning shoppers, and neither were the sort of people who catered to them.

#

An hour later he was only slightly better informed, but somewhat more curious. Albrecht sat on a park bench in front of the library complex, under some local tree sporting fat leaves like green hands with too many fingers. It made for a complex, mottled shade, which he rather enjoyed, despite the stale incense odor.

Well-groomed people strolled by in the pale pastel kilts and blouses that were the local fashion for those with money to shop. None of them looked at Albrecht, which was fine with him. He had time to think and relax a little in the shade before heading down to the reeking chaos of the market to make his day's nut.

Strangely, the keel number had traced to a *Coatimundi*-class fast freighter. Civilian hull type, which argued that the codelock key had been repurposed from its original Naval application. Odd, but not unheard of, especially by people who ran fast and loose at the fringes of the world of certified, inspected, insured commerce.

That class used the old Group 7 c-drives, with the cockeyed Lyne arms that never lasted more than twenty percent of their rated duty cycle without an overhaul—or worse. The keel his codelock key had come off of was originally commissioned as the *Jenny's Diamond Bright* out of Panshin, a system in the Karazov sector almost two hundred lights rimward, halfway across the Empire. Another curious aspect of this business was that *Jenny* was reported lost about twenty baseline years past, in transit between Velox and 4a-Rho Palatine. Also in the Karazov sector. He wasn't up to accurately converting Imperial baseline to local sidereal in his head, but Albrecht figured that couldn't be more than forty years ago local. Thirty or forty years later, an essentially undamaged codelock key shows up in a market two hundred light-years distant from the ship's last port.

He turned it over in his hand. This key didn't look like it had survived a disaster.

Albrecht knew insurance fraud when it bit him in the ankle. Not that it was his business. No one in authority on Halfsummer cared what he had to say about anything anyway. He just found himself wondering how it all worked. Intellectual curiosity was one of his few remaining luxuries.

That was when two men in the dark, bulging kilts and leather coats of Public Safety stopped in front of his bench.

"Been using the library, friend?" asked one of them. *He looks like the smart one*, thought Albrecht—his eyes were more than a thumb's width apart. But in Albrecht's experience, no one who used the term "friend" that way had ever actually acted like they meant what they said.

"Yes sir." Albrecht smiled his dimmest smile. "Checking my mail."

"You get mail, bunny boy?" That was the piggy-eyed one. "From who?"

Albrecht figured he was in for a bad cop/bad cop routine. It seemed a bit much for just sitting on a park bench. "Mail from my copious friends and admirers, okay? Look, I got an appointment. Is there anything else

I can do to help you gentlemen?"

"'Gentlemen,' he says." The smart one glanced at piggy. "Yeah. Come on over to the Public Safety Offices with us. Watch commander wants a word with you."

"Am I under arrest?" It was stupid, he knew, but this was broad daylight in the nice part of town. They weren't likely to beat him senseless in front of the consuming classes strolling the sidewalks.

Piggy snorted. "Not yet."

"Then I think I'll be going." He stood up, smiled, and tried to shoulder his way between the two cops. That lasted about two paces, then Albrecht was on the ground with a shock stick humming in his ear.

"So kind of you to agree to assist us in our investigations," said piggy, leaning over into Albrecht's limited and pain-hazed line of sight. Someone's pastel boots stepped over his outstretched arm without pausing.

#

Golliwog: Powell Station, Leukine Solar Space
Golliwog arrived at Dr. Yee's office door at 05:54 hours. It had been an interesting night, or at least informative. He'd left the library a little too quickly, but eventually discovered that the ident chip in his arm entitled him to meals at the unrestricted dining halls scattered throughout Powell Station.

It was the first time he'd moved unescorted through the public areas of the station. "Public" was a relative term, of course. Powell Station was an Imperial Navy base. Deep Navy, no cooperation with the Imperial Guards or civilian contractors here. Well, except perhaps for Froggie and Old Anatid. Their status had never been clear to him.

Even among uniformed Naval personnel, Golliwog still stood out. He was about two meters, fifteen cents tall, with that certain bulk about him that came from hormone treatments, muscle grafts, and a hideous investment in physical training. But Golliwog could tell from the way other people carried themselves, the way they walked and moved and how their arms swung, that he could have torn any of them limb from limb—even the hard men and women in the dirtside fatigues with the black-on-blue decorations sewn above their pockets. And most of the people he passed clearly saw the same thing. Golliwog moved in a current of muttering silence, always a few decimeters more space around him than the people he passed among gave each other.

He decided he liked the effect.

Now he was in front of Dr. Yee's office, counting the passersby who turned into the corridor, saw him standing there, and remembered sudden business elsewhere that didn't take them too close to him. He was up to seven when the hatch said, "Come in, please," and slid back.

Dr. Yee had never been one of his surgeons. Golliwog's relationship with them had been clear. He was meat, they were talent. He had only ever talked to them to respond to assessments or answer factual questions. "Does this hurt?" hadn't generally been one of those questions.

No, Dr. Yee was—had been?—his cognitive template engineer. She had come and gone through the last eight years of his training, loading routines into his internal systems, testing his effectiveness, tuning his reflexes and pain tolerance.

Golliwog didn't hate or love very much in his life, but Dr. Yee had always brought a certain enthusiasm to her stressing of his systems. Golliwog found himself wondering what last preparations she had for him now, before she signed him over to the Naval Oversight agent.

The doctor's office was much like Yee herself—dark and compact, with glittering, dangerous edges. He walked through a shadowed space where spider-armed machines lurked in silhouette. A hatch ahead stood open, overbright, so that Golliwog had to step from the dangerous shadows into the light of her presence.

Shuddering, he went.

#

It was a while before she bothered to take note of Golliwog. He stood before her desk and patiently watched. Dr. Yee was wearing a uniform, rather than her usual lab coat and surgical smock. Golliwog studied her insignia. Navy, of course, cream white against her space-black skin. Captain, which was a surprise to him. She'd only ever been referred to as "Doctor" within his earshot. But her branch insignia indicated intelligence, not medical.

More interesting to Golliwog were the service decorations he'd never seen her wear before. Yee, all one meter, fifty-five cents of her, was orbit drop qualified. She also wore the tiny red skull of a Marine pathfinder. A hard woman, in more ways than he'd ever imagined, even in his bloody, miserable dealings with her. And in wearing this uniform, she wanted him to be very clear on that.

With a sort of fascinated dread, it dawned on Golliwog that she was the senior agent of Naval Oversight who would be managing him on this mission.

"Figured it out, did you?" She glanced up at him. "I *know* you can go almost seventeen minutes without breathing. Yet even with that much control, I could hear the catch when you realized who your supervisor was. You're going to have to be better, Golliwog, if you're going out in the field with me."

"Yes, ma'am."

Dr. Yee set down her light pen and stared him up and down. "Do you think you could kill me, Golliwog?"

He opened his mouth to answer, then stopped. Dr. Yee didn't waste words, nor effort. She *was* a trap. "I don't know, ma'am," he finally said.

She simply stared him down.

"No, ma'am." *Not yet*, he added mentally.

"Not yet, indeed," she responded, a tiny smile quirking across her face. "Remember, Golliwog, I *built* you. I know what you're thinking before you do. Someday you will surprise me, but not this day."

"Someday, ma'am." Then, on impulse. "That's a promise, ma'am."

She caught his gaze and held it with her own. Her eyes were pit-black, Golliwog realized. "Good." Yee breathed the words out as if she were biting off pieces of her life. "And if you succeed in killing me, then I don't deserve to live."

"Yes, ma'am."

Yee made a flickering gesture with her fingers. The lighting shifted, becoming less harsh, and a station chair popped up out of the deck in front of her desk. "Sit, Golliwog. Let me tell you where we're going and why."

Golliwog sat. Somehow, he realized he had just passed his true final examination.

"Tell me," she said in a voice that was eerily conversational. "I know you've studied ship types. That will be important later. But have you ever heard of a system called Halfsummer?"

#

Albrecht: Halfsummer, Gryphon Landing

He got dragged into the watch commander's office without being strip-searched, which amazed Albrecht. They'd taken his thigh pack, the credits in his pocket, day permit, voided crew card, and the codelock key, and stuffed them in a plastic bag. Albrecht still clutched the receipt chitty.

"Micah Albrecht," said the watch commander. It wasn't a question. She was a big woman, heavy gravity in her genes or a hell of a lot of gym time. She didn't look pleased to see him. Her office was eerily clean, devoid of paperwork, personal decorations, or, really, much of anything but a desk and a single chair with her in it.

So he stood where piggy and the smart guy had left him. "Ma'am."

She stared at him for a while, then shook her head. "People are idiots."

That didn't seem to call for a response.

"You care to explain to me, Mister Micah Albrecht, why I got a hotshot detain-and-question order from an expert legal system looking for people committing insurance fraud on interstellar shipping? With respect, friend, you don't look like an interstellar shipping magnate to me."

So we are all friends here at Public Safety, Albrecht thought. At least he'd guessed right on the fraud, though he couldn't imagine why there was a flag on that data. "I'm a c-drive engineer, ma'am. Old ship types are my hobby. Just reading up."

"Grounded, right? No union card, no engineer's papers." She grinned nastily. "You want to read up on old ship types? Buy a hardbook, read on the can. Stay out of my library and don't waste my officers' time."

He stood, breathing hard, his knees aching from the takedown. At least they hadn't actually *used* the shockstick.

She continued to stare. "Why are you still breathing my air, Micah Albrecht?"

"I'll just be leaving, ma'am." He stepped backward, unwilling to turn away from her.

"Good idea. Don't let me see you again. Ever."

"No ma'am."

Then he was in the hall, being stared down in turn by piggy. The cop said nothing at all, just trailed Albrecht back to the front desk where his belongings were returned, then to the front doors.

It was a long walk to the market, but Albrecht didn't want to stay anywhere near the shade of the fat-leaved trees.

#

He almost threw the codelock key in the trash, but decided to hold off. The tool's presence bothered him. Instead Albrecht headed to the market to find the old Alfazhi trader. The day was heating up and the crowd was thickening as he made his way into the maze of stalls and booths and small-lot auctions. Somehow he expected the old man to have vanished, but the trader was right where he had been the previous day.

"Good tool, ah?" said the trader, looking at Albrecht with a suspicious glint in his eye.

"Yeah. Valve bleeding great." Albrecht squatted on his heels opposite the trader, looking at today's merchandise on the solar sail. More small tools, still the Higgs sniffer, along with a new a collection of vacuum-rated bolts, bindings, and toggles. The spill of an engineering hardsuit's utility pouch, he would wager a guess.

Then he broke the first rule of a marketplace—he asked a stupid question. "Where do you get this stuff from?"

The trader sat very still for a moment, staring Albrecht down. Then, with a shrug: "Here, everywhere, there. Smart man know where look. I sell you, you sell pawn, what difference?"

"Look, I don't care. It doesn't matter. I just want to

know."

"Why you want know if you don't care, ah?"

Albrecht sighed. That was a good question. But the codelock key... something was wrong here. Maybe there was more to it, some angle to his benefit. He slipped a too-precious five-cred chit out of his pocket, showed it to the old man on the palm of his hand, and said the first thing that popped into his head. "I got curiosity like a monkey, ok? My old man, he died on the ship that codelock key came from. I just want to know."

The Alfazhi snatched the chit away. *There went a night's mattress fee*, thought Albrecht. The old man grinned, looking half-crazy now. "Beggar auction."

"What?"

"Dead men, ah? They drink, they die, nobody know them, nobody respect for them, bodies go for reprocessing, stuff go for beggar auction. Not for you, ah. You go now, sailor."

"Yeah." He knew from nobody knowing him. "I go now. 'Ah' to you too." He stood up, wincing from a sharp rush of pressure and pain. That takedown in front of the library was making itself known to him.

"Sailor. One more thing."

"What?"

"Maybe you go down Sixth Wharf. Drink some, talk some. Maybe somebody know your daddy."

"Here? From *Jenny D*?" That seemed dreadfully unlikely. But then again, so did the codelock key, when you got right down to it.

"We live through our fathers, my people, ah. I give you same respect." The trader's face closed into a scowl. "Now go."

#

Menard: Nouvelle Avignon, in transit toward c-beacon 318-f

The Chor Episcopos tried to ignore the angel in his ready room and concentrate on the line of thought that had been nagging at him since his conversation with Sister Pelias. The angel was obviously content to ignore him as it slept, after all. Menard prayed briefly to the power of the Holy Spirit for forgiveness of his unkind thoughts regarding a fellow servant of the Patriarch. Mind cleared and soul somewhat eased, he then considered his situation.

They traveled on the Church fast courier *St. Gaatha*. Being a c-courier, she was a heavy beast. The ship relied on that strange trade-off of mass and acceleration that decreased transit time and energy required to make the transition to a smear of negative matter and perverse equations, resolving some few dozen light-years distant as an allegedly identical copy of ship, cargo and crew. As a heavy beast, she sported large, luxurious cabins.

It was obvious to Menard that his quarters were ordinarily reserved for someone much more senior than he. There was more gold filigree in here than he'd seen in most churches outside the Prime See, and the entire compartment was done over in blue silk upholstery and carpeting, with an ostentation that was just short of bizarre. He had regretfully passed over the ornamented altar with its beautiful iconostasis with Sts. Basil, Gaatha, and Tikhon rendered in delicate brushstrokes. Instead, with a hasty prayer and a careful, sacred kiss, he set up his little traveling icon of St. Niphon with his tiny thurible of Athonite incense.

As strange as his quarters were, they were not so bizarre as the sleeping angel, stretched long and thin with its boots crossed at the ankles. And though Chor Episcopos Menard had made more c-transitions than he could possibly count without resorting to his personnel file, there was still something fundamentally odd about this whole trip. Even without the blesséd angel.

Still, he'd asked to be here. Meant to be here. Following the shiver in his bones and the pricking in Sister Pelias's data.

Even in the face of Menard's interest Bishop Russe had forced the point—something had been driving His Grace, some pressure invisible to the Chor Episcopos but still real enough to affect the assignment.

"Jonah," Russe had said. "This is important. Terribly important. The Metropolitan of Halfsummer will extend you every possible aid and comfort, but that is a rude planet in a rude sector. People who serve on the frontiers don't understand the logic of empire. Or the importance of our work." He'd leaned close, breath reeking of onions. "You will take an angel. To watch over you, and deal with the xenics if you meet them."

An angel. Menard had never heard of one leaving the Prime See, except in the direct company of the Patriarch himself. He certainly didn't need an angel to watch over him. To keep watch *on* him, more like it, in obedience to whatever hidden force Pelias had alluded to and Russe had so obviously been responding to. Politics, of course, to which Menard had too often willfully blinded himself.

And here was the result of his deliberate ignorance of the machinations of power: the angel. It was pale as all its kind—a hairless, sexless creature, close to three meters tall, wearing red leather body armor, with a red Maltese cross tattooed on its forehead. That cross was like a declaration of war to any decent churchman, bloody and wrong. It had no scent, either, except the faintest aroma of leather from its armor. Right now it was sleeping, or least immobile, but when it was alert the solid pink eyes were perhaps the most disturbing. Like the wing of a beetle made from blood, perhaps, with no white or pupil.

This thought came to him: *We find no xenics among the stars, so we make our own to watch over us.*

The angel was an unfortunate fact of life at the moment, but it was not what had been nagging at him. Rather, his thoughts kept ranging to the Internalist position on xenics. Sister Pelias had been quite insistent about her… well, call it intuition. Menard had climbed over, around, and through enough alleged xenic sites to have a thoroughly jaded view of Externalist thinking. To put it somewhat unkindly, he was quite certain that there were no boojums hiding in secret bases at the bottom of craters waiting to either save or destroy the human race.

That being the case, were the Internalists any closer to the truth?

He didn't understand how they could be. Not logically.

Whatever and wherever the xenics might be, if they truly existed—something he very much wanted to be true. Menard *craved* that belief—they hadn't seen fit to announce their existence through leaving behind any conveniently ruined starports or abandoned ship hulls or anything like that. He simply didn't believe that a mature, material, starfaring civilization could have fled before the slow coreward advance of humanity without leaving traces. Consider what humans did to an E-class planet in the course of a few generations. It would take the passage of geological eras to erase the road cuts in inconvenient ridges. Millennia of abandonment to even weather them enough that a planetologist might question the rounded edges.

If the xenics were out there in some kind of physical force and presence, they'd never spent much time on any world humanity had come to occupy or even bothered to survey carefully. He'd stake his ordination on that, though logically he couldn't prove a negative assertion. As the old saw ran, absence of evidence was not evidence of absence.

Of course, when cornered by logic, dyed-in-the-wool Externalists simply shifted the argument. The xenics favored asteroid belts, gas giant moonlets, comets, hard vacuum habitats, whatever flights of science fictional fancy were common that year. But if any of those alternative theories about living arrangements were true, they implied, even dictated, morphologies and behaviors that would be barely recognizable to humans as life. Let alone intelligent actors capable of jiggering equity markets and rerouting comm traffic through their influence—the only evidence, indirect as it was, for xenic presence.

If xenics walked among the worlds of the Empire, the Internalist argument had to be correct, in some form or fashion. And never mind the raging debates over how they stayed hidden, whether they were human in any sense, could they take Eucharist or walk down public streets. As far as Menard was concerned, there was far too much of the human race living outside a state of grace for his peers in the hierarchy to be worried about the theoretical possibility of xenic baptism.

The angel snorted, muscles rippling in its sleep as it interrupted Menard's line of thinking. He overcame his discomfort and stared at it hard.

Canine and equine muscle fibers bundled over spiderweb-reinforced avian bone structures. A narrow braincase not much over 650 cubic centimeters—fatally microcephalic for a human—housing feline-derived neural matter. All that dreadful bioengineering warped into a roughly human shape, of course. Very dangerous creatures.

Doctrine regarded the angels as art, of all things, given that much of bioengineering was quite literally anathema in the technical sense of that term. All the way back to its earliest roots, the Ekumen Orthodox church had an uneasy relationship with technology—God had created the heavens and the earth to be contemplated in pursuit of His glory, not remodeled in pursuit of secular riches. At the same time, a practical churchman was forced to recognize that the business of the Empire would grind to a halt without genetic localization of food crops for varying planetary conditions, not to mention the measures required to maintain sealed environments in space. Nevertheless, the Church had never been at peace with wholesale genetic manipulation. Even biones, with their mainline human DNA, were forbidden baptism and sacraments. Yet these angels were perhaps the most extreme chimeras ever bred by man.

But they were held to be art, like a watered steel sword or a lacquered seat of pain.

Menard hated the things, for all that they were beloved of the Patriarch. The Church Militant had four million men under arms, thousands of hulls, the third largest fighting force in the Empire. Why the Patriarch needed angels was beyond him.

And he wouldn't be able to move a meter anywhere in the Halfsummer system without this thing screaming to the world that he had come from the Prime See, threatening all with judgment and bloody, final absolution.

"Secure for c-transition," the cabin told him in a soothing voice. It was mostly a psychological issue, Menard knew. He'd never noticed so much as water spilled in a c-transition, but body and soul rebelled when the moment came.

The angel slept through the scream of light as they

left reality for points negative.

#

St. Gaatha made Halfsummer space about fourteen elapsed days after leaving Nouvelle Avignon. The ship's systems solemnly assured Menard that eighty-seven baseline days had passed—the objective, simultaneous calendar of the Empire, inasmuch as objective simultaneity could be said to apply over relativistic distances and transrelativistic speeds.

As far as Menard had ever been able to tell, baseline time was mostly used to mark Imperial observances, coordinate military actions, and game the financial system. None of which was particularly his concern. His own lifetimer chip told Menard and his doctors what they needed to know about his biological rate-of-aging.

Aging or not, he was bleary-eyed and stretched. C-transition always made Menard feel as if he'd been inexpertly reassembled. Every doctor he'd ever mentioned it to had sworn the physical reactions were purely psychosomatic.

After kneeling before his icon to give thanks to God for his deliverance once more, Menard meditated a while to bring peace to his heart. Knees aching, when he was done he found his way into *St. Gaatha*'s ward room. This was another large space, pillared like a seraglio, with a sumptuous galley and a vastly ornate coffee engine, all brasswork and valves and shining stopcocks. Someone had thoughtfully bolted a small, plastic consumer-grade coffeemaker next to it, which gave off an entirely welcome warm, brown smell.

Caffeine. He didn't usually take coffee, but it would help knit his miserable joints back together.

"Chor Episcopos," said Lieutenant Kenneth McNally, sitting at the back of a shadowed booth. McNally was *St. Gaatha*'s skipper, a young man with a ruddy complexion and a strangely mobile Adam's apple.

"Lieutenant," said Menard. His mouth didn't feel quite right, either. He fumbled with a stoneware mug and the little coffeemaker, poured himself a steaming cup. The scent alone was worth the trouble, but the way the chilly handle bloomed a little warmer in his palm was comforting as well.

"That monster's gorgeous, and worth a small fortune," said McNally, nodding at the huge coffee engine, "but it takes two people the better part of an hour to produce the first cup. Fun at parties, though."

Stirring his coffee to cool it a bit, Menard tried to work that out. "You have parties on board?"

"Representational work. In port, Chor Episcopos."

"Of course." He sat down opposite McNally. "Tell me, Lieutenant. Do you have a position on xenics?"

McNally quirked a smile. "I try not to run into any."

That answer woke up his lagging synapses. "Pardon?"

"I'm a Freewaller, sir."

"Jonah, please," said Menard, with a vague wave of the hand. "Freewaller… like the battle?"

"Yes." McNally grinned. "Local legend, sir—Jonah. I read your dossier in the public directory. You've spent half your career chasing local legends. Ever been to 3-Freewall?"

"No, can't say I have."

"It's in trailing space. Give us a couple of centuries, we'll be a ghost world somewhere behind the Empire. But we're historic. Still important, for now. Shiploads of tourists coming and going. So many memorials in solar and planetary orbit we have a uniformed service keeping them maintained and on station. Funny place, sir."

"So what's your legend?"

"Asteroids, sir."

He'd heard that one a few dozen times. Ancient ruins tumbling in eccentric orbits out in the Deep Dark. "Externalists, eh?"

"No, not exactly. Within Freewall space, in the right bars late at night, people will tell you the xenics fly around in ships fitted out like asteroids."

That certainly wasn't the stupidest theory Menard had ever heard, but it wasn't going to win any prizes, either. "Doing anything in particular? Or just orbiting with balletic grace?"

"Wouldn't know, sir. I just keep an extra watch out for rocks when I'm making a c-transition run. Just in case there's any moving faster than my ship. Local superstition, I suppose."

Lord, save me from superstition, Menard prayed. *It looks enough like faith to fool the unprepared mind.* "Well, it never hurts to watch for rocks, I suppose."

McNally leaned close. "You ever get to wondering, read the *Ulaan Ude* transcripts. From the battle. Last couple of minutes, when the *Hoxha* blew, right before the old Navy struck their colors to the Imperial fleet. That's what started it all."

"*Ulaan Ude.*" Menard made a mental note of the name, whatever it might mean. He didn't have anything like the right data set with him on this transit, but this certainly was another one of those odd leads that had kept the xenic question alive over the centuries. "Bless you, my son, and my thanks. Creation is ever full of mysteries."

"Indeed, sir. Thankfully my job is to get my ship where she needs to be, and fulfill the mission requirements of the run as a whole."

Menard smiled at the other man's tact. "The 'run as

a whole' being me and my nanny."

"Well, yes. We're a fast courier. People usually aren't that anxious just to see their paperwork, so mostly we carry VIPs." The Lieutenant crossed himself. "Holy relics, sometimes."

"And sometimes those are one and the same, eh?"

McNally grinned. "Nothing like a Churchman, Chor Episcopos."

"Nothing like."

"Indeed. Look, do you want to come up on the bridge in about twenty minutes or so? We've already done our initial postarrival orientation. We're ballistic right now for a systems shake-down and crew wake-up, but we'll be pulling the beacon chatter, setting our course toward the inner planets and so forth. If you'd like to observe."

Menard sipped his coffee. Advantage of a small ship, he supposed. "I wouldn't want to be in your crew's way."

"Oh, don't worry about that," McNally said cheerfully. "We could probably hold midnight mass on *St. Gaatha*'s bridge."

#

Albrecht: Halfsummer, Gryphon Landing

It took him almost a month to work up the nerve to go down to the Sixth Wharf. He had to make mattress money every day. Most days he made food money as well, sometimes he ate his seed money. It was a losing game. The whole time, Albrecht hung on to the codelock key. He'd taken a beating over this, by damn that made the stupid thing his. He had been avoiding the old Alfazhi in the marketplace, though. The bugger was too strange by half.

Somehow the Sixth Wharf was never far from Albrecht's mind.

Eventually he had a day where the morning came

too soon and he was actually a few credits ahead of his never-ending financial game.

He decided to go looking for *Jenny D*. It was something to do, some direction to take other than this endless circling at the bottom of a well of both poverty and gravity.

The Sixth Wharf was a riverside dock. It was haunted by the watermen who moved barges up and down the silted, hummocked swamps extending hundreds of kilometers around Gryphon Landing. As far as Albrecht was concerned, countryside was the colored stuff around a spaceport, but these men lived among the creeper vines and the large, carnivorous cousins of the hand trees that dotted the city. And watermen hated spacers, with a sort of genial venom borne out of the mists of history.

Nonetheless, there he went dressed as only a spacer would be, in his grubby shipsuit and his thigh pack. The wharf was a narrow boardwalk street footing a set of docks jutting out into mold-green water that looked to have the consistency of insulating gel. There were only a few boats tied up, but the docks were covered with ropes, boxes, piles of rusted junk, all of them spilling into the right of way. Grubby and messy enough to give any starship section supervisor heart failure.

He walked along, breathing in the heavy scent of the river. Just after sidereal noon, none of the few people idling along the Sixth Wharf seemed to be in a fight-picking mood. The regulars must be out doing whatever it was watermen did by daylight by way of earning an honest living.

The first bar he came to was The Newt Trap. Walking in, there still didn't seem to be anyone in a fight-picking mood, so Albrecht spent two more precious credits on a swamp beer from a dispenser and stared around at the walls a while.

If this place had a theme to its decor, it eluded him. It certainly wasn't particularly nautical. There was a stuffed newt chained to the ceiling, one of Halfsummer's three-meter monsters with a terribly oversized mouth full of sticky, pointed cartilage. The walls were practically covered with a mess of everything from old sweaters to children's toys to flattened ration cartons, all nailed or wired tightly in place.

"Man goes out on a long cruise, he leaves something of his own to come back to," said someone behind Albrecht in a voice that squealed like low gears under poor lubrication. "To draw him home."

"I get it," he replied, still gazing at the walls, wondering at the sick-sharp sweat smell.

"Easier places for a vacuum-brain to drink than a wet sailor's bar. About midnight, you'd get your nostrils slit just for being in here."

Albrecht turned to look his new acquaintance over. The man was fat, in a way that you never saw in space. Planet fat, gland disorder fat, eyes buried in folds of skin like cold-burned rubber, tiny hands on the end of arms that puffed wider than both of Albrecht's thighs put together. He was wrapped in a damp muslin winding that made him look like a badly laid corpse. Several badly laid corpses smashed together, in fact.

"Don't matter to me," the newcomer said in that grinding voice. "I ain't no waterman neither. But if you're looking for something, might want to find it before the barges come in." He grinned, a disturbing effect given the apparent lack of teeth and wide, blackened tongue. "That would be starting around 16:30," he added helpfully.

What the hell, thought Albrecht. He wasn't made of money or time. He might as well ask. "Ever hear of a boat called *Jenny D*?"

That drew a long quiet stare. Then: "Funny question, that." The fat man settled in to the bar next to Albrecht, a process not unlike docking a water boat. "*Jenny D*'s kind of, oh, a virus around here. What's your connection to her?"

The lie carried on. "My father died on that ship." As far as Albrecht knew, his father was alive and mean as ever back on I-Karlstein.

The fat man crossed himself with three fingers. "He's in good company, your old man."

Albrecht let that thought ride in silence a moment before asking, "What kind of virus?"

"Deadly. It's catching. Too much talking brings it on. Frankly, we'd like the whole thing to go away." He gave Albrecht a long stare. "You the kind of man who can make it go away?"

Time to leave, Albrecht thought. Getting tripped on the pavement by cops was one thing, but whatever people were dying—or killing—for down here on the docks wasn't his cup of tea. "Uh…."

"'Uh' is right." The fat man smiled again. "You ain't nobody, ser. You ain't a waterman, you ain't Public Safety. Maybe you'll do, without drawing too much fire down upon all our heads." A great, shivering slab of a hand patted Albrecht on the arm. "Tell you what: Since you asked, I got something to show you. For your late father's sake."

He slid away from the bar and waddled out into the sunlight. Albrecht downed his swamp beer and followed. That intellectual curiosity was still nagging. Besides, if this came to nothing he could always head back to the market and scrounge for more junk to resell.

#

"They build here…" The fat man puffed hard as he walked, bobbing slowly along, sweating rivers. "By digging…" Puff. "Then sticking something…" Puff. "Down a hole…." Puff. "Caisson." Puff. "You know that word?"

Albrecht wanted to ask the fat man to stop, to breathe, to talk in sentences, not to keel over onto the wooden street next to him like three hundred kilos of bad vat-flesh. "Yeah. Pressure vessel, right?"

"Right." Puff. "But anything that…" Puff. "Will hold out the…" Puff. "Water table…" Puff. "Will do." Puff. "Anchor the found…" Puff. "…ation to."

"Right." Inasmuch as he'd ever thought about dirtside engineering, that made a certain muddy kind of sense. Starships didn't have foundations, but they had keels and hull frames.

They drifted to a stop in front of a godown not much different from the meat rack where Albrecht spent his nights. Maybe a little rattier. A few more posters on the walls, not pulled down by the owners or the Public Safety work crews. The fat man leaned against a door and let his chuffing breath idle down to something almost human. After a while he smiled that black-hole smile again and opened the door with a mechanical key. "Come on in."

Inside wasn't particularly large for a Gryphon Landing warehouse, but it was particularly empty. Albrecht looked up through the cross-braced girders to a roof full of bright holes. Shafts of sunlight speared through, becoming grubby in the dusty air. A slightly rippled quality to the shadows between the bright, glimmering columns promised a truly astonishing number of flittermice come dusk.

"Space," he said. "But not my kind. Aren't these buildings usually full of… something?"

"Sometimes a building is just a building." The fat man waddled slowly across the empty concrete floor to a little office framed in at the back corner of the godown. Albrecht trailed after, wondering what a human being had to do to reach that kind of end state. The thought was sobering.

The fat man opened the door, then stood aside.

Albrecht looked in. Two desks, some file cabinets, a ratty old rug with three chairs parked on it.

"Throw back the rug," said the fat man. "Then tell me what you can do about *Jenny D*."

Armstrong's ghost, this was nuts, thought Albrecht. He scooted the chairs aside and flipped back the rug. Not much to his surprise, there was a trap door. He glanced at the old man, then tugged at the inset ring.

The door opened more smoothly than he'd imagined it would. Below was a shaft, like a wooden chimney. Iron rungs were set in one side. Albrecht shrugged. "You got a light?"

The fat man said, "Glow stick in the desk, maybe."

Albrecht tugged open a couple of drawers to expose various nests of pens, tools, and a very ancient sandwich ascending its own private evolutionary ladder before he found a pile of glow sticks. He stuck several in his sleeve pocket, snapped one, bit it gently between his teeth, nodded at the fat man, then began climbing down.

Nothing ventured, nothing lost. It wasn't like he had much left to lose, either.

He wasn't the least bit surprised when he found a vacuum-rated hatch at the bottom of the shaft, hull vanishing into a damp darkness in each direction from the opening in the shaft. The access pad with the oversized suit glove keys had been torn out and replaced with a little hand-wired codelock interface.

"*Jenny D*," said Albrecht, mumbling through the glow stick. "As I live and breathe. Two hundred lights from your lost grave."

He might not know much about killings and dockside life, the issues that had worried the fat man, but he knew ships. Albrecht set the codelock key against the interface and watched the hatch of the buried ship swing inward.

#

Menard: Halfsummer Solar Space
The Chor Episcopos didn't usually travel by fast courier, just hopped whatever Church or commercial hauler was headed wherever he was going.

The concept of too much space on a starship continued to strike Jonah as odd. Yet here was an enormous bridge, with dozens of duty stations and enough floor space to host a low-gee badminton tournament. McNally hadn't been kidding about being able to hold a midnight mass. And the entire space was occupied by McNally, two harried ensigns, and Kewitt, the ship's elderly chief petty officer who seemed to be mostly sleeping.

"He's handling the on-course station keeping," McNally said, following the line of Menard's gaze. "Rock watch. Things too big for our clearing masers or defensive nano to cope with."

"With his eyes closed?"

"Yes. He's tracking nearby junk on audibles. System control's already got us on our assigned trajectory inward from the c-beacon. They preload those, of course, but they're not fine-corrected. Kewitt's keeping an eye on our progress through immediate localspace."

For some reason, Menard found this amusing. "Listening for xenics. Keeping an ear, as it were."

"Exactly."

The Chor Episcopos nodded, looking at the main screens. *St. Gaatha* had a triple bank. One showed a schematic of their current course, distance-distorted for casual viewing to collapse the projected eleven-day transit toward the inner planets. Another showed a distance-corrected system plot, while the third displayed an animated flyby of the Halfsummer system.

Halfsummer-α, the primary, was a fairly typical G2 star. Classic human-friendly, and therefore precious. The solar system was also stereotypical, four inner E-class planets, an asteroid belt, with one super-J, two J-class, and one sub-J standing outside the belt. Only one of the rockballs was solidly within the Goldilocks zone—the world of Halfsummer itself. The others weren't worth the bother of terraforming, though there was some mining activity scattered around all three of them. Fairly clean system, from a junk perspective. Kewitt's rock watch spoke more to the Lieutenant's caution, or superstition, than to any outstanding local traffic hazards.

"Permission to speak freely, sir?" McNally said, disturbing Menard's thoughts.

"Of course," said the Chor Episcopos. *More rocks*, he wondered?

"I've made, oh, thirty runs as skipper on the *St. Gaatha*. Another sixty or so as a junior officer on three other rotations. And... well... I've never carried an angel before. Never even seen one up close before yours came on board."

Menard thought that over, decided to let the question of who controlled whom lie fallow. He'd said too much previously as it was, and did not want to project disrespect for his superiors in the hierarchy. "Mmm?"

McNally sounded distressed. "Why... why am I bringing an angel to Halfsummer? What have these people done?"

Ah ha. "Rest easy, Lieutenant. The angel is my security detail."

"You planning to start a war, sir? Or possibly stop one?"

"I really can't say what I'm doing here." Not even if I knew what that was, he thought. "But no, no wars. Nothing dreadful."

McNally crossed himself. "Thank you, Chor Episcopos."

"We are each servants of God, my son," Menard said kindly. "Both the word and the blade are His tools in their time."

"I'm an officer of the Church Militant, sir. I am sworn to this." McNally glanced over his shoulder, aft toward where the angel slept. "But some things don't feel so godly to me."

Menard couldn't have agreed more, but he wasn't in a position to say that now. The Chor Episcopos ignored the tweak in his gut. "We all move at the Lord's will."

McNally's usual smile flickered back across his face. "Mysteriously, at any rate."

#

Golliwog: In c-space

Though Golliwog had been on dozens of ships of many sizes and ratings for training exercises, he'd never before left the space around Powell Station. He had been through simulation after simulation of the dangerous period of emergence from c-transition, when a lack of human alertness and an inherent unreliability in ship's systems placed vessels at risk, but no one had ever warned him about what happened *during* c-transition.

Unbuckling the safety straps, Golliwog smiled into the colors. The hatch of his cabin was some infinite, purpled distance from his bunk. What luck his legs were infinitely long. He had trouble fitting his planetary fingers to the hatch controls. It was easier to step through the bulkhead. The wind of his passage thundered a hard, dry lemon.

The passageway outside was uncomfortably thin,

bulkheads as close as Casimir plates. Something was wrong with the dimensions. But Golliwog tunneled between them like a decaying alpha particle, looking for Dr. Yee.

He found her soon enough, a puddle of plaid improbability in a roiling maw of cayenne that was probably her cabin. He wasn't sure this was how c-transit was supposed to work. Golliwog looked around the echoes of her workspace until he found something that tasted like paper. A stylus took longer, though he finally decided the cold pressure near the paper-taste might be it. Golliwog wrote "WOKE DURING C-TRNST TRIED TO REACH YOU—G", then drifted among the wounded stars back to the infinite reaches of his personal universe, where sleep reclaimed him brutally as any surgeon on a deadline.

#

Menard: Halfsummer Solar Space
After a polite but boring period watching the bridge crew watch their screens, the Chor Episcopos retired to the ward room to work. He'd been avoiding his ready room, even though it was part of his quarters, because the angel had spent the entire journey thus far lurking there.

Menard knew that art or no art, anything with eyes and a brain certainly qualified as one of God's creatures. It was a trial set before him to love, or at least respect, the angel. Had Bishop Russe possessed anything resembling a sense of humor, Menard might have believed that his supervisor had set the angel upon him as a reminder of the Chor Episcopos' own failings. But McNally had been correct in his fears for Halfsummer— angels never traveled away from the Prime See, except when the Patriarch took it upon himself to conduct a peregrination. The creatures went wherever His Holiness traveled, of course, scouring evil so that His Holiness's feet might tread only on sacred ground. Their wrath was legendary.

Enough, he thought. He was being uncharitable at best. Menard offered a small prayer for forgiveness, then looked at the dataslate on the table in front of him. Once she'd shifted down from c-space, *St. Gaatha* had followed ordinary procedure and done a beacon interchange. The vast majority of that process was highly standardized information, read-writes of updated shipping schedules, various sorts of low-priority news and information from the last beacons she had passed by, as well as dropping off and picking up whatever mail was needful. Being a Church ship, she didn't go through the rounds of time-dependent information auctioning that were a basis of a major portion of the Imperial economic system. A complex interplay of scarcity, distinctiveness, demand, degree-of-confidence, and timeliness governed a multitrillion-credit-per-year futures market that the Church considered her flight crews to be above.

What the Treasurer-General did to manage the Church's fortunes was another matter entirely, of course. Menard didn't doubt that some expert system deep in the bowels of the ship's small-scale nöosphere had been auctioning off commodity and political-legal futures data since they'd first dropped out of c-transition. That activity simply wasn't conducted on behalf of *St. Gaatha*, her crew or passengers.

As for the mail, since *St. Gaatha* had moved ahead of her own information wavefront in heading for Halfsummer, no one knew they were coming. Therefore neither the ship nor Chor Episcopos Menard had any individually addressed messages waiting. There was a small classified Church packet, which Menard took upon himself to review.

There were a handful of parish report summaries intended to be passed along to the Prime See. He ignored them. There were three disciplinary files, also of no interest to him. He marked them anyway, in case he found sufficient idle time before planetfall to go back and check whether any of the troublesome priests had been found to be xenics in disguise. There were a whole series of financial logs, which would probably bore him beyond tears, but Menard felt that he ought to analyze for anything reflecting Sister Pelias's K-M curves. Finally, there was a security report with a route flag that included the Xenic Bureau.

Curious, the timing of that. The hand of the Lord, or the xenics finally showing themselves as more than data ghosts? With a slight shiver of his spine, Menard went to the security file first.

Somewhat strangely, it was a copy of a Naval intelligence message. Beneath the Church codes, the message itself was in clear text. Also stranger, but useful as well, since he didn't have any way here aboard *St. Gaatha* to crack Naval codes. Menard couldn't tell from the headers whether the message had wound up in Church files as an intercept or a friendly tip-off—that sort of thing varied wildly from system to system, as well as depending on the vagaries of budget battles and political tension.

#

> To: NINO Front Royal/New Bellona/Front Royal
> Fr: NILO Front Royal/Gryphon Landing/Halfsummer
> Re: Shipping Watch List Flag
> Burt—
> Be advised we had a data flag trip on the shipping watch list here. Keel

number PNSH017λFA2900045661, registered IBY57 as *Jenny's Diamond Bright*, lost IBY98 in transit Karazov/Velox to Karazov/4a-Rho Palatine. We looked into it, some visitor checking keel histories for his model collection. I know you hate coincidences, so I'm forwarding his file to you, but I'm certain there's nothing to this one. My love to Roger and come visit sometime. We can go wetwater sailing on Southport Bay.

—Alma

#

The message was a lot more interesting for what it didn't say than what it did say. Menard doodled on his slate, decoding.

NINO was Naval Intelligence, Naval Oversight. NO were the hard men inside the Imperial Navy, a combination of internal affairs investigators, system auditors, and hit teams. Burt, whoever he was, would be a tough nut indeed if Menard ever ran across him.

NILO was Naval Intelligence, Local Observer. Someone named, or code-named, Alma. Who probably had a certain amount of local authority, as in "we looked into it," but could be anyone from the portmaster to a clerk in the city government. The Church didn't have a role corresponding directly to LOs. Parish priests were, by definition, everywhere, and made for terrific coverage, even if providing a somewhat spotty reporting network.

Obviously Alma and Burt were old friends. He wondered whether that was significant to the issues at hand.

What the message didn't elaborate on was the identity of the visitor, where he was visiting from, how he'd tripped the flag—nöosphere search would be the obvious choice—nor did it say how Alma had made her investigation, and what had been her degree of confidence in the outcome. Menard presumed that most or all of that info was in the missing file attachment.

More significant to the Chor Episcopos was the fact that one of the classic xenic phenomena was disappearing ships. Father Bernie O'Halloran ran a statistics unit that reported up to Sister Pelias, reviewing shipping losses across the Empire. O'Halloran's extracts tended to be of greater interest to insurance investigators than to his peers at the Xenic Bureau, unfortunately. But Menard was here at Halfsummer looking for xenic anomalies, and by goodness the missing *Jenny's Diamond Bright* was a bona fide potential xenic anomaly. He felt that chill of inspiration once again. Much like the apparent opinions of the NINO operative named Burt, Menard felt that sheer coincidence would be too much in this case.

Menard composed a note to the Bishop of Halfsummer introducing himself and his credentials, and requesting help from the Bishop's staff in locating Alma's model-collecting visitor.

As he sent it off to be transmitted in-system as part of *St. Gaatha*'s datastream to the Halfsummer nöosphere, he looked up to find the angel standing behind him, silent as cold death. How had it gotten there? A long-fingered white hand, nail red and narrow and gleaming, stabbed past his shoulder to land on the name *Jenny's Diamond Bright*, nearly cracking Menard's dataslate in the process.

In spite of himself, Menard jumped in his seat. His scalp crawled with fright as his spine shook.

"Please—" he began, then stopped. He had to control his reactions to this red-eyed monster. It was his tool, seconded to him by Russe, and by hierarchs far above the Bishop, to be sure. Tool or no tool, there was no negotiating with angels. By definition. They were the Lord's slaughter weapons of Ezekiel 9:2, made flesh by the modern word of man. They could only be directed by the hand of the godly.

And this one was not aimed at him. No matter what the gurgling fear in his bowels said.

He tried again: "I understand. This is a priority for me, too. We serve the same ends, my s-son."

The angel glared at him, red-eyed and vibrating, then slowly nodded before stalking out of the ward room.

How had it known what he was doing? The thing hadn't stirred from his ready room in the days since they'd boarded.

Menard called up his favorite passage concerning space travel, from Psalms 19. "The heavens declare the glory of God;" he read aloud. "And the firmament shows his handiwork. Day unto day utters speech, and night unto night shows knowledge. There is no speech nor language, where their voice is not heard. Their line is gone out through all the earth, and their words to the end of the world. In them hath he set a tabernacle for the sun."

He knelt to pray a while, for peace and wisdom, guidance on the matter of the angel, and, if the Lord were especially kind this day, a greater insight into his purposes here at Halfsummer. His knees spoke louder than God, but Menard found peace amid the tingle of incense and the words sent toward Heaven.

#

Albrecht: Halfsummer, Gryphon Landing
The buried ship wasn't *Jenny D*. Albrecht realized that

by the time he cleared the inner hatch. *Coatimundi*-class freighters weren't atmosphere-rated, for one thing. They dumped cargo cans at stations, or lightered their manifests down if need be. *Jenny's Diamond Bright* would have been hard-pressed to make a hydrogen skimming run through the upper wisps of a J-class planet. Not to mention she would have been a lot bigger than the hole underneath this godown could possibly have fitted.

No, thought Albrecht with a substantial measure of satisfaction, what he had here was one of *Jenny D*'s boats. Still substantial proof she hadn't gone missing on the Velox run—not that he cared too much, he wasn't a fraud manager. More to the point, this little vessel was something he could pilot on his own.

Too bad the boat was sitting under a few hundred tons of building, foundation, and associated landfill.

He made his way forward, to the bridge. As this was a boat, not a ship, space was at something of a premium. The power-to-weight issues for vessels that confined themselves to nonrelativistic distances would have been familiar to an early Industrial Age engineer back on old Earth, using only a pocket computer to design steam locomotives and so forth.

He found a three-seat flight deck, hard shields secured over the view ports. It was clean, all instruments in place. That suggested that the rest of the boat likely hadn't been gutted for salvage either. Even stranger, ready lights blinked to indicate systems on standby.

Who would bury a spaceship, then leave it turned on?

Someone the locals didn't like, obviously. Or the fat man wouldn't have brought him here.

How was a more pertinent question. It wasn't that great a stretch to imagine landing a cutter in a hole in the ground—he'd bet this was a *Shostakovich*-class or similar, not more than thirty meters in length. It *was* a great stretch to imagine landing a cutter in a hole in the ground within port-controlled airspace without that event being taken notice of. Unless somebody had ensured a groundside sensor blackout, for maintenance or training purposes. Even at that, dozens or even hundreds of people equipped with nothing better than a human eyeball would certainly notice a boat dropping out of the sky in the middle of a developed area.

It was not a subtle thing to do.

Using the codelock key, Albrecht lit up the crew workstations. The boat had power. It had actual, live system power. A feed from the city mains, probably. It's how he would have done it. A commercial–industrial area like the Sixth Wharf had all kinds of big customers with weird consumption profiles—a standard two-kilovolt industrial feed would keep a boat this small live and warm on long-term hold.

A few minutes fiddling with the control panels made things clear enough. This boat was *Jenny's Little Pearl*, a *Xiao-Gang Ye*-class cutter—very similar to the *Shostakovich* series. The boat definitely thought it had touched down about eleven years ago, though Albrecht wasn't the least bit prepared to trust the log. *Pearl*'s systems were at 61% of optimal, which was pretty damned good for something that had been sitting underground for years. No killing failures, though redundancies left a lot to be desired. And it had almost fourteen hundred hours of fuel load, bloc hydrogen stored in ion-lattice sponges. Enough to go skiving around Halfsummer's inner system, if the boat could get into the air and out of the gravity well in the first place.

So now he could turn it off and go back to his five-credit mattress. Or he could stay on board and eat freeze-dried chow and wait for someone to come find him. Or he could try to figure how the boat was supposed to get back out from under here. As the fat man had said, make it go away.

As if there were any question what he would do next. This wasn't as good as being back on a c-transit run, but it was hell of a lot closer to space than he'd come since being busted off *Princess Janivera*.

Time to start tracing circuits, Albrecht thought. The bad guys would find him if they wanted him. They probably already knew where he was.

Before he got to work, Albrecht dismounted the hotwired hatch controls and locked himself in.

#

Four hours later he had eaten a very bad bag of something that was allegedly chicken fried rice, and established several key facts about *Jenny's Little Pearl*. The boat was indeed on the city power mains. He couldn't see the billing interface from inside the power shunt, but Albrecht would bet his left foot the power authority didn't know where that particular five-kilovolt line was terminated. The same umbilical that brought in power brought in a ten-millimeter water line, which kept environmental systems sufficiently hydrated without needing to draw down ship power in order to crack water out of the air. It also brought in a local nöosphere link, which meant *Pearl* had a comm number and data access.

Somebody had wanted to be able to send out for pizza.

And they had, at that. Pearl had four cabins, two port and two starboard. The portside cabins, closest to the hatch, had obviously seen use as cells. There were literally chains welded to the bulkheads. Albrecht wasn't too keen on examining the stains on the decks in there. The starboard cabins had a more lived-in look.

This boat had been a prison and a hideaway both. Not a bad method of keeping out of sight for extended periods. Store a few ships of food upstairs, skim some off for provisions down below; with the unmonitored utility feeds, no one would ever know.

Damn lousy waste of a good ship's boat, but at the same time, Albrecht had to appreciate the ingenuity involved.

It wasn't the only ingenuity on board, either. He also found a soft control stack loaded in the engineering panel, which was highly customized and utterly uncommented. Albrecht traced the circuit routings and eventually located a second outside connection down in the engineering section—a hand-built job that didn't strike him as very trustworthy, but there it was.

In effect, the unmarked control stack was a big red button labeled "Push Me." Either you were supposed to know what it did, or you weren't supposed to push it. Albrecht figured the control had to launch some process that extracted *Pearl* out of the hole in the ground—somebody had gone to a lot of trouble to keep her up and spaceworthy—but he was darned if he could see how the boat was supposed to get out. Blow up the godown and lift from the crater? Any explosion powerful enough to shatter the poured concrete floor upstairs would seriously endanger the boat.

He decided to ask for an opinion. Albrecht used the command panel to open up a generic nöosphere access and asked for a connection to The Newt Trap, along Sixth Wharf.

"Thank you for calling The Newt Trap," said the bar's comm system, displaying a sort of titchy fractal screen saver.

"I want to talk to—" Albrecht stopped. What was the man's name? "The fat man. You know the fat man?"

"There is no one here by that name."

Damned machines. Any human would have known exactly who he meant. How many four-hundred-kilo monsters could there be hanging around the Sixth Wharf? "Let me speak to a live person, then. Anyone."

"Please wait." The comm switched him over to a syrupy hold music that went on for about two minutes before the screen flickered and the fat man came on.

"Oh... it's you," he said. "Enjoying yourself?"

"More fun than a barrel of junkies," Albrecht replied. "I think I can make your problem go away, but I need to understand something."

The fat man's piggy eyes narrowed to flickering slits. "What would that be?"

"Someone wired this thing to leave. If it can find clear air, the right hands can make it go away for good." He flexed his fingers in front of the pickup. "Mine, for example. But what happens when I press the go button? I don't see how it works."

"You don't—" The fat man cut himself off, glanced at something out of the pickup range. When he looked back again his eyes had narrowed, his face pale. "Go now, boy. They're coming." The connection dropped.

Albrecht sat and thought that one over. Less than a minute later, the boat's systems warbled. Someone was trying the hatch.

"Guess you got my address," he told no one in particular. "Time to press the big red button." He initiated hot-start preflight sequencing from the command panel. It would take about twenty minutes to get *Pearl* ready. Unless his visitors had brought a thermic lance or some serious machine tools with them, they weren't getting in that fast. Not now that he'd secured the hatch.

The command panel bleeped. Incoming comm link.

He tried to imagine a downside to answering. Whoever was out there knew he was in here. The fat man wouldn't be hard to sweat. Public Safety had already shaken Albrecht down once, a month or so ago after the library incident. If they had been following him around, they knew it was him, and they knew he was down here.

If it was the bad guys, whoever they might be, well... same logic. No one was getting in without some damned hard work, and he wasn't coming out now. Albrecht felt oddly cheerful. It was sort of like jumping off the cliff and hoping like hell there was more water than rock under that mist down there.

He answered the call about the time a dull banging began echoing through the hull. "*Jenny's Little Pearl*, flight deck."

A hard, familiar face flickered into being on the panel. Of course—it was the Public Safety watch commander who'd briefly interrogated him those weeks ago.

"Oh," she said, almost sadly. "It *is* you. I've just lost a hundred-credit bet."

"Hello, ma'am," said Albrecht with a sort of preternatural cheerfulness. If he didn't get *Pearl* into orbit quite soon, he was going down so hard and so far he'd have to tunnel up to find a shallow grave. "I'd make it up to you if I could."

She leaned into her pickup, eyes large and bright on his panel. "What the hell are you doing? I'm getting screamed at from several unexpected directions, my little ship type collector. I can't even get a decent trace on this comm number yet. I don't know if you appreciate how truly annoying that is for someone in my position."

"So it's not your goons knocking down my door?" Albrecht asked, surprised.

"Micah Albrecht, I don't even know where your door *is*."

"Hmm." Was there harm in telling her? "Might want to get a rapid response team down to The Newt Trap. It's a waterman's bar down along the Sixth Wharf."

"I know the place." She glanced away, catching the eye of someone out of his view and nodding. Then: "You're not there, are you?"

"Close by. Let's just say bad people knocked over The Newt Trap a few minutes ago looking for me."

"Black Flag," she muttered, then looked away from the pickup again and shook her head before returning her attention to Albrecht. "What about you?"

Black Flag, he thought. *Of course*. No wonder the fat man had been worried. Vicious anarchists, one and all, with deep pockets. Albrecht had never understood what they wanted. It might explain how this boat had wound up under a building. Their kind of move, slick and clever and undetectable. But the cop had asked him a question. "It seems I've accidentally landed in the middle of your insurance fraud problem. Despite not being… um… what was the term? An interstellar shipping magnate?"

She looked interested in spite of herself. "Do you plan to survive the experience?"

The echoing bangs intensified. Serious machine tools it was, perhaps. "We'll both know in about fifteen minutes. In the meantime, if the fat man tells you to duck and cover, I'd listen very carefully."

"Listen…." She closed her eyes and sighed, then shot him a hard glare. "I'm Public Safety Lieutenant Alma Gorova. You live long enough to tell more of the story, you call and ask for me. I'll listen."

"You're about to know a lot more than you realize," Albrecht said. "That's a prediction, not a promise, but I'm standing behind it with my life."

"Good luck, Micah Albrecht. Don't do anything I'll have to kill you for later."

"My fondest wish, ma'am."

When she signed off, Albrecht amused himself by arming the antipersonnel defenses around the main hatch. About fifteen seconds later, the banging on the hull stopped.

He had thirteen minutes to go. That time went by without further terrible ado, and with a relieving absence of additional distressing comm links. Albrecht kept a close eye on the hot-start protocols and on the upward and downward jumps in systems readiness. All he had to do was make orbit. Then he could effect repairs if need be. He tried not to think about hunter-seekers running him down. Surely the Halfsummer system had never bothered to arm to that degree?

When the hot-start was ready, Albrecht put it on ten-second hold, then shifted to the engineering panel. He looked at the anonymous, jerry-rigged control again, then initiated its sequence.

The damned thing didn't even have a password. It just kicked off a wailing alarm as something began to boom loudly outside his hull. He lit up all the screens and watched *Pearl*'s structural integrity very carefully.

Much to Albrecht's amazement, hull sensors showed outside pressure and temperature changing. He toggled through various external camera views until he found something visible.

Water was rushing in around the hull. He could feel the deck rocking slightly.

That wasn't ideal, but it wasn't immediately disastrous. More to the point, why? He studied the screen. All he could see was shadowed water and foaming mud. Something fairly large surged in and clunked against the hull.

Wood.

"Oh, crap," Albrecht whispered. He called up the nöosphere window and searched for a map of the Sixth Wharf. *Zoning overlays*, he thought.

Light bloomed on the viewscreen. Sunlight. Outside air.

What the hell had happened to the godown above his head? Obviously this was *Pearl*'s escape process, but what was he supposed to do?

The control stack on the engineering panel warbled its ready state.

Ready. Yeah, right. As far as he could tell, he was still under a building. Igniting *Pearl*'s atmosphere drives would simply destroy ship, building, and Albrecht in one go. But here was light, and water.

The nöosphere showed him the requested zoning overlay for the Sixth Wharf. He toggled for historical use. And there it was, the godown four buildings west of The Newt Trap. It was built on top of an old dry dock.

Pearl was sitting in a dry dock. A real one, the original kind, not the metaphorical sense of the word as applied to a Level Three ship maintenance facility. A dry dock, at that, which had just flooded.

So… he powered up the gravimetrics, an inversion of the artificial gravity systems that managed inertia during space maneuvers and doubled as a taxi system under g force. That gave him slight positive buoyancy. He then applied one half of one percent thrust, portside reaction clusters, parallel to gravity plane only. That would shift the hull toward the breach in the foundation wall. Locks, he thought they might called. There was a lot of debris floating in that water, judging from the camera feed. The boardwalk street must have collapsed when those locks opened.

He powered up. *Pearl* rocked. Something groaned

as whatever had secured her pulled loose. On the viewscreen, water boiled and steamed in response to the thrusters. He wasn't doing the building any favors, but at least he wasn't blowing it sky-high.

Albrecht steered the reaction clusters on dead minimum power, moving the boat toward open water outside the locks. And this, of course, was how they'd gotten in here, he realized. Landed it somewhere out in the swamps, beyond approach control's oversight, then steered or towed it through the waterways and on into the dock. Which probably already had a superstructure framed over it to hide *Jenny's Little Pearl*. Do the whole operation late on a Saturday night, close the locks, drain the dry dock and bring in enough bracing and fill to hold up the floor above, finish the building, secure and power down the ship—a secret hiding place, physically safe, with its own built-in escape mechanism.

Much simpler than shutting down approach control, as he'd first theorized. Damned clever, in fact. But then whoever had been maintaining this thing had been a little too hard-nosed among the watermen, until the locals' hatred had finally trumped their natural secretiveness.

All his screens lit up. The boat was now riding low in open water, out in sunlight. Albrecht opened the view port shields as well, but all that did was let in the light.

From the hull cameras, he had several odd-angled views of the docks. There was a hell of a ruckus going on out there. A riot, really. He spotted Public Safety troopers in ballistic armor, water sailors swinging tools and hooks, and a whole lot of ordinary people fighting it out. *Pearl*'s sensors helpfully highlighted several knots of people in chameleon suits. That would be whoever had tried to break into his hull, he figured. A few people were shooting at him, but there was nothing in that crowd that would make a dent in an atmosphere-rated hull.

But he couldn't light up his drives out here, either. He'd cook several dozen people minimum, and possibly set fire to the docks. All of them. So Albrecht upped his reaction cluster power a few points and steered for open water, ignoring the shuddering as he ran down slow-moving waterboats.

In a few minutes, he'd have enough clearance to fire off his drives and lift out of this damned gravity well. Assuming approach control didn't call down an orbital interdiction strike or something equally drastic. Once he was in orbit, there would be new problems, but a one-horse planet like Halfsummer wouldn't have much in the way of gunboats with which to run down miscreants like himself.

He hoped.

#

Golliwog: Halfsummer Solar Space

Dr. Yee found him a few hours after the ship emerged from c-transition. Golliwog had been violently sick upon returning to realspace, and too weak since to clean his spew.

She looked around his cabin briefly, then stared into his misery. "It doesn't affect human beings, you know."

"Not human," Golliwog croaked. "Bione." His systems all checked normal. He was pretty sure a medical scan would show his physiology within baseline tolerances. That the inside of his mind could be this disrupted frightened him.

"Of course. It doesn't affect biones, either." Dr. Yee's expression softened slightly, for a moment. "The universe is a dangerous place. Dangerous places sometimes call for dangerous people. Which leads me to wonder how suitable you really are, if you can lie there groaning."

"Ma'am." Golliwog reached for his straps.

"You left me a note."

"I did?" He tried to remember doing that.

"I assume it was you. You appeared to sign it."

"Appeared, ma'am?"

"Do you remember anything about the c-transition, Golliwog?"

"Colors," he blurted.

"Colors?"

Golliwog found his feet, towering two heads taller than the woman who held his life at her word. "Colors, ma'am."

"No one remembers c-transit. Ever. It's widely known to be an instantaneous process, relative to one's personal timeline. But strangely enough, I believe you."

He wiped the spew off the front of his shipsuit. "Thank you, ma'am," he said in a very quiet voice. The world was much stranger than even he had imagined.

Yee waited until Golliwog was finished cleaning himself before touching his elbow. "I want to show you something."

"Ma'am."

He followed her into the passageway, which seemed oddly spacious for some reason Golliwog couldn't quite parse out. They walked forward a few meters, and into her cabin. She waved him to her workstation.

Her dataslate's screen was furrowed, plowed like a muddy field, with a note. It read, "WOKE DURING C-TRNST TRIED TO REACH YOU—G."

"I don't know anyone on this ship who would have thought to enter my cabin," Yee said. "It's widely viewed to be a terminal experience. Perceptive crew, these sailors. You, however, possess a combination of naïveté and familiarity sufficient to take that risk.

"I am further at loss to explain how someone even with your powers and skills could carve cultured diamond lattice. That would ordinarily require industrial machine tools." Golliwog realized Yee was nervous—he'd never seen her rattle on quite like this. She continued: "And the furrowing effect, as if the diamond had been liquid. This…" Yee tapped the slate, "is why I believe you." She leaned in close, her breath hot against the bottom of his chin. "*How*, Golliwog? *How?*"

"I… I don't know, ma'am. I don't remember."

"It's important. Very important. I suggest you consider remembering. When we are done with our business here in Halfsummer, we shall investigate this most thoroughly."

Golliwog shrank inside. "Investigate" to Dr. Yee meant going back inside the world of labs and clinics and operating rooms. Possibly for the rest of his life. Which might not be long at all.

The unfamiliar seed of protest lodged in his heart. Golliwog was smart enough to say nothing.

"As to our business here on Halfsummer, I expect to be updated shortly on local conditions. You should spend some time in the ship's gym, as we may soon be transferring to a fast boat."

"Yes ma'am." Golliwog saluted and left. A workout would give him time to think and burn away some of this newfound fear and anger.

#

Later, Golliwog watched a virteo in the ship's tiny closet of a training room. It was a roughcut of various security feeds and system control records, documenting the whys and hows of starship disappearances—hijackings and insurance scams for the most part.

He knew his combat ship types, but civilian vessels were a blur to Golliwog. All the talk of switching keel numbers, hacking transponders, and IFF codes was logical enough, but it wasn't sinking in very well.

People do wrong, Golliwog thought. That idea had never made sense to him back on Powell station. There were attackers and defenders, people to be supported and people to be eliminated. That one might deliberately violate a regulation had always seemed something between stupid and suicidal, especially on a ship or station.

But he thought he was beginning to understand wrong. Breaking ranks. Running away. Ignoring orders.

He was afraid of what would be done to him, because he'd damaged Dr. Yee's slate.

Maybe those people who stole starships were afraid, too. Was fear the basis of wrongdoing?

Golliwog was fairly certain that someone somewhere understood this question, but it wasn't him. Then the virteo caught his attention again, with an image of ragged men in ragged shipsuits being slammed against a bulkhead by a squad of Marines in combat armor. Some of the slammings looked fatal to Golliwog's practiced eye. Not that he needed the power assist of combat armor to do that to someone.

"...Black Flag, routed from a hideout in the belt of the Feodora system," said the narrator. "These criminals proclaim a political agenda, but financial gain is very clearly their highest priority. In the past five baseline years, the Black Flag has executed over two thousand innocent...."

His attention drifted again. Hiding in a belt. What could a Golliwog do on his own in an asteroid belt? Not much. But those men had stolen ships, protected themselves.

No matter, he told himself. It was an impossible thought. Dr. Yee was his controller, and thus she would remain.

But what could someone who walked during

c-transition do to a ship?

He folded that thought away along with his fear, and watched a discussion of dark beacons and c-transition navigational diversions on the virteo.

#

Menard: Halfsummer Solar Space
CPO Kewitt woke the Chor Episcopos from his doze in the ward room.

"Sir," said the old man without a trace of irony. "You've a priority message in the comm queue, sir. From His Grace. The Bishop of Halfsummer, sir."

Menard's eyes ached with sleep and the pressure of blood where his face had been pressed against his dataslate. "Fine," he said, stifling a yawn. His breath smelled like stale coffee. Only one cure for that—more coffee. "I'll look at it immediately."

"Can I get you some coffee, sir?" Kewitt asked.

"That's alright, Chief. I'll fetch it myself." Menard stood, wobbled slightly, then made it to the little coffeemaker. It was still percolating. Percolating again? How long had he been asleep?

"Very well, sir." The elderly CPO left. Menard got new coffee, sat down, tried to see whether the angel's red, stabbing fingernail had damaged his dataslate. Surely he hadn't dreamt that? *Oh Lord*, he prayed, *preserve me from my own fears*.

Fear was perhaps a greater enemy of faith than superstition, after all.

Message. From the bishop. Menard squinted at the timestamp on the slate. He'd only sent his message about four hours previously. Allowing for lightspeed lag from the outer system, that meant that the bishop, or someone on his staff, had responded almost instantly. He called it up and read.

#

To: Chor. Ep. J. Menard/St. Gaatha/In Transit
Fr: Diocesan Offices/Gryphon Landing/Halfsummer
Re: URGENT re Your inbound message

Chor Episcopos—

I pray for Your Reverence's blessing and beg forgiveness for this hasty, too familiar correspondence. Speed seemed to be of superior virtue to etiquette in this matter, given the content of your recent message, specifically its reference to a starship known as *Jenny's Diamond Bright*.

A major incident broke out two days ago along the water docks here in Gryphon Landing. In a peculiar coincidence, a boat from the ship you named in your message seems to have been involved. The local authorities permitted the ship to make an illegal departure rather than engage it on the ground in an inhabited area. The Imperial Resident has ordered orbital defenses to intercept the wayward boat. Our poor solar system's one Naval Reserve light cruiser is currently in the process of being deployed to that end.

His Grace advises that if you have an interest in this *Jenny's Diamond Bright* you might wish to put whatever influence you have to bear toward breaking off the current pursuit. His Grace further offered several colorful metaphors regarding the chances of the rogue pilot surviving the intercept.

I hope this letter finds you in health.

—The Priest Enxo Danel, Amanuensis to His Grace the Bishop of Halfsummer

\#

Saints and martyrs, thought Menard. A ship had finally come back from the dead. Or at least a ship's boat. Maybe Sister Pelias's K-M analyses were paying off. It was certainly an anomalous event, whatever the likelihood that there was to be xenic influence somewhere at the heart of it.

Menard shivered. And then there was the angel's interest in *Jenny's Diamond Bright*. If "interest" was the appropriate term for the sort of fatal intensity usually associated with being an angel's focus of attention.

He couldn't allow that boat to be overhauled and destroyed. "Currently in the process of being deployed" was vague but ominous. Menard flipped the dataslate to ship's comm and buzzed McNally.

"I'll be right in there, Chor Episcopos." The lieutenant was as good as his word, making it to the ward room a minute or so later. He looked crisp but slightly hurried as he stepped up to Menard's station chair and visibly suppressed a salute. "What can I do for you, sir?"

"Do we have any authority here in the Halfsummer system, Ken?"

McNally's look became a stare. "Chor Episcopos?"

Menard sighed. "Do we have any authority here? Practical authority, to intervene in an impending military action by the locals?"

"Uh… no. Strictly speaking, no. Sir."

That wasn't the first such opening Menard had ever

heard in an official conversation. He caught the toss. "And *not* so strictly speaking?"

"Well... *St. Gaatha*'s a fast courier. Not a warship as such. But all vessels of the Church Militant are armed, sir. For the greater glory and to be of full service to the Patriarch. According to our files, the only armed vessel stationed here is a pre-Imperial light cruiser with a reserve crew. She outguns us by about a hundred gigawatt/seconds of nominal firepower, but our weapon systems have a century's worth of engineering improvements, and much better range."

"So that's authority through superior firepower."

"Yes, sir. Unfortunately we're still about fifty transit hours from being in effective reach of any action occurring in Halfsummer planetary space. We do of course have the moral authority of the Church, especially with Your Reverence's presence here." McNally pitched his voice down. "I assume the Bishop of Halfsummer would be in accordance with any actions we might take within his diocese, of course."

"Of course," murmured Menard, fascinated. McNally had all the makings of a politician. He'd already realized that the lieutenant was more than just another Church Militant missilehead, but even so, it was a new side to the man's character.

McNally held up two fingers. "Authority through force, authority through moral suasion." He lifted a third. "We also have authority through misdirection."

"Excuse me?"

"We're not a civilian ship. We don't dump our files out to information auction when we hit the system. Some of them, yes. But not en masse. So you can send a message to the Imperial Resident or the Naval Reserve commander asserting authority over the fugitive ship. No one will be able to contradict you, since *St. Gaatha*'s systems have the most current information in Halfsummer space. Only we know the truth. I assume this regards the *Jenny's Little Pearl*, yes?"

"Yes…." Menard was still processing the concept of authority through misdirection.

"Excellent. Tell them you've got an Edict of Attainder against the vessel and its crew. The Bishop can manage the local arguments if you're using the authority of the Prime See."

"That would absolutely constitute bearing false witness," said Menard in a faint voice.

"Not if you swear one out. This is a Church courier, sir. We have a Patriarchal Seal in our ship's locker. For just such emergencies. There's a procedure in Church Militant regulations for the Hierarch on the scene to swear out an Edict by proxy. That would be you, sir. As long as the Bishop endorses it, the Edict will be valid here in system. If there's a challenge, the canon lawyers can argue about it later back at the Prime See. You might wind up in Ecclesiastical Court someday, but meanwhile, you've asserted legitimate authority in pursuit of the mission assigned you by the Patriarch. Which *St. Gaatha* can back with force of arms, sir."

"You're a dangerous man, Lieutenant McNally," Menard said after some thought. He needed that boat. He needed that pilot. "I predict you'll go far."

McNally bowed his head. "Perhaps, sir. I have been counseled in the past on my need for humility."

"Park the humility 'til we're done pushing around the locals, Ken."

"In that case, sir, you might want to commence your misdirection with an immediate transmission. We're still over ninety light-minutes from Halfsummer planetary. You'll want your Edict there as soon as possible. I can assist you with the Seal and other formalities after the fact."

"Bless you, my son," said Menard.

"Thank you, Chor Episcopos. I live to serve."

"As do we all."

#

Albrecht: Halfsummer Orbital Space

"Get off my ass!" Albrecht screamed. It wouldn't do much good, but it made him feel better. The main screen plotted the merciless hours of his demise.

He'd spent the better part of two days in a hyperbolic orbit, avoiding defense satellite footprints, bolting down the various bits of equipment that had broken loose during his departure from beneath the soil of Gryphon Landing, and reprogramming the boat's systems to respond to him. There had been a variety of threats and entreaties via comm, both of which Albrecht had ignored in equal measure. The lightly armed orbit hoppers that provided screen defenses to Halfsummer Station didn't have the range or speed to catch a ship's boat powered for systemwide operations.

All he had to do was avoid them.

But now the locals had scraped up a God-damned Naval Reserve light cruiser so old it probably burned fossil fuel. The beast had lurched into action from Halfsummer Station about forty minutes previously, presumably after shaking off a few tons of rust.

Given that his boat's entire armament consisted of a single two-gigawatt/second meteor popgun and an empty weapons locker behind the bridge, it didn't matter how crotchety that light cruiser was. Once she found a solid vector on him and put on some thrust, he was done for. The probability curves that *Pearl*'s systems were calculating had a progressively unpleasant trend.

He should have gotten underway a day ago. But there'd been the shorts in the gravimetric system, which really hadn't been designed for immersion in brackish water. He wasn't willing to undergo full acceleration with dodgy inertial compensation in place. And the water tanks were having all kinds of weird valve problems, which affected their utility as heat sink, radiation shielding, and mass distribution compensators. *Jenny's Little Pearl* must have sucked a bunch of crud through some autocycling intake while he was wallowing around in the swamps prior to takeoff. At some point he was going to have to purge the filters and strip the valves. As it was, the whole boat stunk of moss and mud.

And now the Imperial Resident was throwing the local Naval Reserve after him. How pissed could these people be?

The comm squawked, then issued the shriek that meant a military priority signal. "*Jenny's Little Pearl*, this is Lieutenant Svetlana Bourne, commanding officer of the INRS *Novy Petrograd*. Please acknowledge our hail."

He flicked a control on the main panel. "Bugger off, *Petrograd*."

There was about six seconds of lightspeed lag. "It's Micah Albrecht, isn't it? Look here, I've got a shoot-to-kill from dirtside. You don't want that, do you?"

Albrecht set himself a course toward The Necklace, what the locals called their asteroid belt. It was faintly visible at night from the surface of Halfsummer, a silver thread across part of the sky, and as a destination set his pursuers on a stern chase. May as well not make Bourne's job any easier. "What do you think?"

Another lag, long enough for him to reflect on the value of being a smartass to the person who would be soon holding a gun to his head. Then: "Well, neither do I. Certain fire control officers on my ship notwithstanding."

"Lieutenant, what the hell did I do? Launch without clearance isn't a capital offense, and I know I didn't kill anyone." The dirtside newsfeeds had been clear enough about that, though there were some irritated boat owners and dockside businesspeople down there. "I can make a reasonable claim for this boat being salvage. *I* certainly didn't steal it from its rightful owners. Why the temper tantrum?"

He rechecked his course, waiting for her reply, then began to consider the job of stripping the filters and valves from the tankage.

"My opinion? You got the wrong people arrested. Some of them have powerful friends."

That was true enough. There were a lot of people in custody due to his little waterfront adventures, and some of them were quite angry about it. He'd apparently broken open a local cell of the Black Flag while making good his escape. There were some surprising names on that list of anarchist revolutionaries, sending hard ripples through the local politics of Gryphon Landing.

"But my opinion doesn't matter," Bourne continued. "My orders do. And my orders require me to intercept you and your ship, and bring you both into custody. With a shoot-to-kill instruction if you do not render full cooperation."

"Come and get me," said Albrecht. He killed the priority comm job with an engineering override, and went to find the filters. With the course set, *Pearl* could fly herself in her last few hours of life. The least he could do was keep her in proper shape.

#

He worked in the cross-passage that connected the port and starboard passages immediately forward of engineering. The main tankage lines ran right above that passage, managing mass and volume distribution between the primary tanks in the boat's flanks and the secondary storage in the dorsal and ventral hull sections. Albrecht had set grippers on the filter access panel, which was unaccountably placed higher than his head at an acute angle to the deckplane and the relevant gravimetric field. Even low-priority systems required maintenance, a little fact that seemed to consistently escape the attention of low-bid naval architects and shipyards across the empire.

That meant when Albrecht backed the last of the torque screws off, it was going to want to fall, pretty much on his head. Maybe the designers had intended zero-gee maintenance for this system, but he needed his burn speed enough that he didn't want to shut the gravimetrics back down.

The power driver took the six torque screws out one by one. With each screw the panel settled a little, releasing more of that mud smell. Whatever goop the boat had sucked in had, naturally enough, gone to the filters.

The panel groaned as the last screw came out. Albrecht flipped the switch on the lower grippers, which should have caused the panel to swing forward, hinging on the upper set.

Instead it burst loose as something large, wet, and furious dropped on him, amid a sheet of warm, stinking water.

Albrecht slammed down on his back. Jaws wide as his shoulders snapped in front of his face as something massing at least a hundred kilos bounced on his chest. He stabbed with the torque driver. It squealed, bit his left wrist, butted him in the groin, then scuttled through the open hatch into the port passage.

"Christ on a mass converter!" Albrecht shouted at the overhead. "What the hell was that?"

He was afraid he knew, though. It was two meters at least, maybe three, and heavier than he was, with a mouth full of familiar horror. He'd seen his last newt hanging from the ceiling in the fat man's bar. Now he'd seen his next, still alive and biting.

Albrecht caught his breath. "Boat, secure all hatches," he said, gripping his wrist with his right hand to control the bleeding.

"Secured," said *Pearl*.

"Where is it?"

"Where is what?"

"*It!* Um… a hundred kilograms of mobile biomass. The lizard with an attitude, you idiot."

"There is an unknown party in the portside passageway."

"Don't let it out."

"Acknowledged."

Could he vent the air there? Not in a boat this size, it wouldn't have the kind of vacuum-rated compartmentalization of a larger ship. *Princess Janivera*'s smallest single vacuum-rated area had been considerably larger than the entire interior volume of *Pearl*. He could maybe gas the damned creature, but that would require some environmental control tricks that weren't Albrecht's specialty. Besides which, he wasn't sure this boat could handle something like that.

That steward's nephew would have come in handy about now, he thought. The little bastard could either have killed the newt, or he could have been fed to it.

"I need medical attention," he told *Pearl*. "Please initialize the sick bay systems."

"Acknowledged."

#

He decided to let the newt rampage for the time being. There wasn't much he needed from the portside passage.

Since that was where the primary airlock was located, it was also the most likely boarding route for whoever Bourne sent after him. Assuming she didn't blast *Jenny's Little Pearl* to scrap and haul Albrecht back to Halfsummer in a number of small plastic bags. Let some Marine reserve sergeant meet that thing head on, angry and hungry as the jarhead came through the lock. Albrecht wouldn't be surprised to see the big bastard bite through combat armor.

Of course, the damned mud-and-crud smell was truly everywhere in the air system now.

The probability curves on the main screen had narrowed considerably. *Petrograd* had a turn of speed on her, for an antediluvian warhorse. He had maybe four hours to go as a free man. At least he would go out as master of his own vessel, even if it was only a system boat.

Albrecht decided to amuse himself by pretending he had a future. He started by sorting through *Pearl*'s log, looking back before the grounding date when the boat had been settled in beneath the godown on the Sixth Wharf.

Astonishingly, nothing was there.

He ran a debug trace on the memory cores. Logs were write-once, for all kinds of very good reasons. The only way you got a blank log was if someone ripped all the black boxes out and replaced them. Which was almost a capital offense, also for all kinds of very good reasons.

There was exactly one entry in the log, before the grounding date. Albrecht studied it.

It was an ephemeris, a detailed position-in-time record for an object in an eccentric orbit that intersected The Necklace at regular intervals. Nothing but the orbital plot, no notes about what was being plotted. A really good astrogator might have been able to work out mass constraints based on the orbital variance reflected in the plot as the object interacted with The Necklace, but that was beyond Albrecht.

He'd bet good money he was looking at *Jenny's Diamond Bright*. Though that was a damned strange orbit to park a freighter in. Obviously, someone hadn't intended it to be found.

Had the whole purpose of hiding *Jenny's Little Pearl* been simply to provide safe storage for that ephemeris data? The boat, in effect, as key to the missing freighter. The codelock key he'd bought in the market was key to the hidden boat.

And someone had been mugged, or died in their sleep, and lost that codelock key to the gray market of junk and resold tools. Even to an apolitical civilian like him that was an obvious drawback to the kind of cell systems the terrorists used... it was hard to manage succession of responsibility and chains of custody. He could only imagine the fury of the Black Flag, or whoever had stolen and hidden this boat, at losing track so thoroughly of something so important.

They must have been staking out the warehouse down by the water for a long time. Hoping to get their codelock key back. Albrecht wondered whether the fat man had called the Black Flag in on him.

No, those lunatics had to be the deadly virus the fat man spoken so elliptically of when Albrecht had mentioned the name of the ship.

And a ship *Jenny D* was. If he somehow survived Lieutenant Svetlana Bourne and her flying mortar of a light cruiser, he could finally have a shot at getting out of this damned system. He'd need to pick up some crew—no starship could be flown solo. But there had to be hundreds of busted-out, stranded, or retired c-rated spacers in The Necklace.

Albrecht looked at the probability curves again. The intercept cone was slowly turning into an intercept line.

#

With an hour and a half to go, the comm bleeped again. Bourne, wanting to talk. His wrist throbbed and burned, he was hungry, and he was going to die soon. Might as well talk. Albrecht flicked her into being. This time he got video as well as audio.

She was pretty, in a sort of aging-elf way. Curly white-blonde hair, narrow blue eyes, a Naval uniform cut for someone ten kilos heavier. Behind her in the camera pickup he could see a couple of ratings working on a spaghetti of wiring.

"Calling to gloat, Lieutenant?"

Comm lag had shortened, too, he noticed, though she'd probably anticipated his first words. "You're an interesting man, Micah Albrecht. You have enemies, or possibly friends, in high places."

"Excuse me?" Enemies he could believe, but Albrecht had become remarkably short of friends lately. He wondered whether he could count the newt.

Again, she was leading him a little, speaking even ahead of the lightspeed lag. "You and your vessel appear to have come under a Patriarchal Edict of Attainder. Which trumps even my orders."

Albrecht's heart skipped several long, cold beats. "If it's all the same to you, I think I could see my way clear to surrendering now." He could imagine a lot of things he'd rather do than be dragged off by goons from the Church's Security Directorate. Which was pretty much what that Writ of Attainder had to mean.

They killed people with toothpicks. And worse.

Her smile crisped into being some seconds later. "I don't blame you, Ser Albrecht, but you've had your chance. I must yield to the tender mercies of the most excellent servants of His Holiness. If it's any consolation, I shall continue to shadow you in your travels as an observer on behalf of the Imperial Resident."

His bowels gurgled. "They're coming for me *now?*"

Another shorter-than-lag response. This woman was *good*. "Inbound from the Trivagaunte beacon. Forty hours out of Halfsummer orbit, perhaps. I'm transmitting their course profile. Purely as a courtesy, naturally. I don't suppose you'd consider standing to and awaiting the arrival of your new pursuers."

"Uh… no thanks." The Trivagaunte beacon was about a hundred and fifteen degrees around the ecliptic from his current heading. God seemed to have just given Albrecht a few more days of freedom.

This time she waited out the entire message lag. She had been giving him a chance. "Well, I thought not. It's been a pleasure serving you, Ser Albrecht. May I say good luck."

He was a dead man sailing. May as well keep heading for The Necklace. Maybe some other even higher power would intervene.

Albrecht wasn't a praying man, but he wondered whether this was time to start.

#

Golliwog: Halfsummer Solar Space

"Someone has called up the Reserves." Dr. Yee was furious. Golliwog could tell by the way she paced, with a twitch in her step. Her arms were clenched behind her. The three ship's officers in the briefing room shrank in their station chairs. None of them would meet his eye, but then, none of them had met his eye the entire voyage. The air dampers in the ceiling were clicking madly, trying to ionize the air and scrub out the stress hormones.

A holographic rendering of the Halfsummer system spun slowly over the conference table. It was distance-compressed, the courses of relevant ships rendered in Dopplered color vectors to indicate degree of compression. Golliwog could see three ships of interest: their own heavy cruiser, INS *Dmitri Hinton*; a Naval Reserve light cruiser—a *Ciudad Boise*-class ship, from a very old keel series long since decertified for active service—and a civilian boat.

The boat was heading for the Halfsummer system's asteroid belt, the light cruiser tailing but not overtaking. *Hinton* was on an intercept from c-beacon β005-a, locally known as the Feodora beacon. Their least-time course involved arriving at the civilian's belt destination some nine hours after both the civilian and the Reserve cruiser were there.

Yee paused in her pacing, a finger stabbing down toward the display. "That was bad enough. Someone else *then* interdicted the Reserves. That, gentlemen, is worse. We look incompetent in the eyes of the locals. We draw attention to our purposes here, and to the Navy's involvement in events." She stared around the table, finally settling her glare on one luckless officer. "Commander Marek, you will interface with the Naval Intelligence local observer here on Halfsummer and determine whose idiocy has put our movements on center stage of this system's newsfeeds." Her stare shifted. "Captain Hawking, I'd very much appreciate a fast boat at our disposal. Golliwog and I need to be at the course intercept point prior to the civilian's arrival."

"Yes ma'am," said Hawking and Marek together.

"Go."

They went, leaving behind Lieutenant Spinks. He straightened up, brushed off his cuffs, and smiled at Yee.

"You've put the fear into them, Suzanne."

Yee sniffed. She still looked angry to Golliwog, but he could see her relaxing already. "Motivational," she said.

Spinks glanced pointedly at Golliwog. Golliwog stared back. Spinks resembled Yee… small build, big eyes, very dark, very tough.

"He's mine."

"Yes ma'am." Spinks gave Golliwog a quick wink.

So, thought Golliwog. They weren't that much alike. *That* was something he'd bet his left thumb Yee would never have done. But still, a connection.

"*Jenny's Diamond Bright*," snapped Yee, obviously picking up a prior thread of conversation.

Shaking his head, Spinks said, "Not with that drive trace. A system boat. Quite possibly off *Jenny D*. Too much of a coincidence not to be connected. But public newsfeeds aren't naming ship names right now and we haven't got a packet from *Novy Petrograd* or the NILO yet."

"Is the big girl here, though?"

Spinks once more glanced briefly at Golliwog. "We've been over that, Suze. Time and again."

"She's *somewhere*, night take her." Yee stepped closer to the hologram, stared into it as if wisdom might be found there.

"Maybe…." said Spinks. "Maybe. That's an inconclusive analysis at best."

The worm of rebellion stirred once in Golliwog's heart. He spoke up: "What analysis?"

Yee snapped him a glare as Spinks grinned. "We're looking for a missing ship," she said.

"*Jenny D*?" Golliwog asked.

"No. *NSS Enver Hoxha*."

Golliwog had never heard of that ship. He wasn't

even sure what an NSS designation was. He gave Yee his blank look.

She sighed. She knew him too well. "*Artemis Powers*-class battleship. One of the old dictators, from the pre-Imperial Navy."

"There is no battleship class in service," Golliwog said.

"Precisely. Do you see the problem?"

Golliwog thought that over. "That class must have mustered more than two hundred terawatt/seconds of firepower, to be considered a battleship. More than four times the throw wattage of anything in service now. And big. Right?"

"Big," snapped Yee.

"Long-lost as well," Spinks added. "Most of us who work on these problems consider it a permanent loss. Best it stay that way."

Yee whirled on him. "But what if you're *wrong?* What if it's out there somewhere? What if the Black Flag or some third-generation Republican cell gets their hands on it? Or just a run-of-the-mill shipping mob, for Armstrong's sake! It would take half the fleet to stop one of those old battlewagons. And we could break the Navy's back trying."

She was talking a lot. That meant she was angry again. "How do you know it's here?" asked Golliwog.

Spinks caught Golliwog's eye, shaking his head slightly. "She doesn't, my friend. No one does. If we knew, we'd have caught up to it long ago. We worry because a ship like that could restart the Civil War. All the other dictator-class ships were broken up after the Long Parliament dissolved, under His Imperial Majesty Ivan the First. *Enver Hoxha* was reported lost during Second Freewall. The question hinges on the fact that no one's ever found a large enough debris field to account for her mass."

Golliwog was fascinated. Someone had lost an entire battleship. *If a battleship could disappear, maybe he could too*, whispered a traitor thought. "Stolen?" he said.

Spinks shrugged. Yee sat down, tapping the table with a light pen, then glared hard at Golliwog. He knew this wasn't about him, so he just stared back.

"*If* someone has her," Yee said slowly, "and they were refitting her with materiel from any kind of cash or traded market, we'd know. You couldn't hide that much movement of mil-spec equipment and parts. Even the black market leaves traces. So, deep in the back offices of Naval Oversight, we track correlations on several trends. Ship disappearances and excess yard capacity are two of those trends. Lost ships have lost cargoes, and the missing hulls themselves can be stripped for parts. Yard capacity could mean refits under way, possibly in bits and pieces." Her pen cracked against the tabletop. "There's a *lot* of excess yard capacity in Halfsummer. There's a historical overage of shipping losses in the Front Royal sector in general. And just lately, one of the ships on the loss list seems to have made a reappearance here." She waved the shattered barrel of the light pen at the hologram. "Her boat is currently being very publicly pursued, but not overhauled, by the Naval Reserves. Simultaneously drawing attention to the boat in question and emphasizing the Navy's role. As well as our apparent ineffectiveness."

Yee grinned. "We don't like to look bad."

"No, ma'am," said Golliwog. He wondered who the poor bastards were on that boat, and if they knew how much trouble they were in.

#

Yee and Spinks spent the next forty minutes going through

a seemingly endless round of minutiae regarding ship movements, ratios of parts and tool tonnage to shipping tonnage maintained, and other logistical detail. They seemed to be tapping Halfsummer's nöosphere for local records, at a deeper level of detail than whatever edited summaries found their way into Naval Intelligence archives elsewhere in the Empire.

An ensign sidled through the briefing room hatch, saluted in a state of near-terminal nervousness. "Captain's compliments, ma'am, and there's a fast boat ready."

"Has the engineering crew stripped our hull codes and transponders?"

"Ma'am, yes ma'am."

Yee glanced at Spinks. "Keep at it, Jan. Tell me what I need to know when I check in. Golliwog, you've got five minutes to be dressed and ready, civvies and class three armament, boat deck. Go."

Golliwog went.

#

The boat deck was big, cold and empty. Golliwog could see his breath fogging. There was a massive hatch in the floor, and an overhead crane system folded up against the ceiling. The whole space was a great white agglomeration of machinery, workstations, and lockers, whispering with an echoing hush. It was confusing to the eye, too uniform in color and complex in form to be easily processed, except for the recognizable boats clamped into cradles around the margins of the boat deck—two cutters, a yawl and a runabout. One cradle was empty, and a slim, black boat sat on delicate runners atop the hatch.

He studied her. Golliwog didn't recognize the hull type. Admittedly, identifying ships and boats by external observation was a rare skill—not often did a person get a good, clear view of the outside of a ship under way, and stationside you mostly saw hull curves or individual nacelles rather than entire shape.

This was a strange one, though. She was black, with no visible markings. The reaction thrusters and drive pods had a strange profile, to reduce the range at which they could be detected, he presumed. She bulged to the aft, which implied an oversized power plant. Fast, stealthy, and undergunned, or perhaps completely unarmed.

He was the boat's weapon system, of course.

Class three armament was the only gear that would pass a civilian security scan. No power packs, no obvious blades. That left him with breakable plastics in his grooming kit, wire stiffeners in the lapels and boots of his shipsuit, and a number of useful cords woven into the seams. Still, over a dozen distinct weapons, plus his barehanded skills and his well-trained ingenuity.

In a way, Golliwog had always preferred working without energy weapons or kinetics. They were effective but graceless. Class three was *personal*.

The civvies went with the weapons profile. There was no hiding that he was large, and dangerous. So Golliwog went with a ballistic cloth shipsuit in a formal cut, with a carbon-leather skidracing jacket. With his bald head and height, it made him look like the dockside thug in any of a thousand virteo adventures.

No one truly threatening bothered to look this threatening. That was the theory, at least. Golliwog was unconvinced of its effectiveness. He'd never been on a civilian dock, not in his life. It would be a new experience.

Could a bione hide on a civilian dock?

He waited a while for Yee, almost fifteen minutes. Golliwog had made the deadline, it was up to her to set the next move.

I am a weapon, he thought. *I await my trigger*.

When she came, she was bright to the point of absurd. Yee had traded her uniform for a swirling, smooth fabric of a dozen or more colors, and a matching headdress. She looked like a walking explosion, rendered in textiles.

"Ma'am," said Golliwog.

"The less said the better," Yee growled. A hatch on the black boat folded open. "Get in. You're driving."

He got in. He drove.

#

Menard: Halfsummer Solar Space

"*Jenny's Little Pearl* is running for the asteroid belt, Chor Episcopos."

Menard looked up from his contemplation of a data dump out of the Halfsummer nöosphere. "Wasn't she doing that before?"

"Yes." McNally grinned. "Looks like our Naval friend, *Petrograd*, told him the good news, then backed off to see what happens next. We're not getting direct transmissions yet, but the information wavefront is close enough to adduce this from observation."

"I think I know who Alma is. There's a Public Safety watch commander in Gryphon Landing by that name. She's got her fingers all over this. *Pearl* made a big mess bugging out dirtside. There's been something approximating an abortive coup going on down there. The Imperial Resident has declared martial law."

McNally snorted. "Over a boat launching?"

"Black Flag's involved." Just saying it gave him the chills. If the xenics were the hidden, maybe-real terror out there in the Deep Dark, the Black Flag were the all-too-real terror that sometimes came screaming into the light, guns blazing, fighting against rational order.

"I see. We're chasing xenics, not terrorists, right,

sir?"

"The Black Flag is no friend of the Church either, my son."

"They're hardly xenics, though."

"Someone would have noticed." *Right?* Menard sighed. Analyzing this sort of thing was his entire life's work, and it still sometimes gave him a headache in short order. "How are we set to intercept *Pearl*?"

"Not before she makes the belt," said McNally unhappily. "I'd much rather overhaul in open space."

"And there's never such a bunch of libertines and free-thinkers in any solar system as your average belter. They're about as likely to listen to that Edict of ours as they are to sprout reaction jets and float away."

"Yes, sir."

"You think much about insurance, Ken?"

"Insurance, sir?"

"On shipping. Somewhere at the bottom of the current dustup here on Halfsummer there seems to be an insurance scam. Something that might well show up on Sister Pelias's Kenilworth–Marsden diagrams. I'm trying to connect insurance scams to xenic activity."

McNally chewed that over. Menard watched as the Lieutenant's Adam's apple bobbed up and down a while. Finally: "Why in the universe would xenics want to run an insurance scam?"

"If I could answer that, I might have a piece of the truth."

"With respect, Chor Episcopos, you need more sleep."

"The angel's moved back into my cabin, Lieutenant. I think it wants me awake and thinking."

"I'll put on more coffee then, sir."

Menard bowed his head in thanks, then while he was there decided to pray a while for wisdom.

Why had the angel focused on the missing ship?

\#

McNally and Kewitt tucked into a pair of steaks while Menard continued to work. He'd prayed long enough it felt like a nap, thankfully off his knees, though Menard experienced a vague muttering of guilt over that. There was sense of elusive thought in the air that he wanted to pin down before resting for real. The smell of food was bothering his stomach a little, especially the vile tangy sauce that Kewitt seemed compelled to squirt all over his meat.

"Did you know," said Menard, trying a fact on for size, "that they have a blessèd huge shipyard in the belt here? For refitting ore trains and comet tugs, supposedly, but this market analysis from the University of Southport says it will take two generations to recoup capitalization, and will almost certainly be obsolete before that point."

Kewitt paused between bites of gristly protein. "Big comets, Your Grace?"

"I am not My Grace," Menard answered mildly. "You may call me Chor Episcopos if you wish to be formal, Chief."

"He knows that." McNally favored Kewitt with a sidelong glare. "Been listening to too many rocks. What do you make of it, sir?"

"I don't make anything of it yet." Menard considered nuking up a dinner for himself. "I just find it interesting."

"Whose money?" asked Kewitt through another bite of steak.

Menard flicked a few screens along his dataslate. "Belt consortium. Small investors, big dreams."

"Making a bid for independence," said McNally. "Slip a few gunboats in the build line, buy off any inspectors or reporters that happen by. This system isn't armed worth a da—Excuse me, Chor Episcopos. This is an ungunned system, that antique the Naval Reserve has flying around out there notwithstanding. They're building hulls."

"What about the Black Flag?" asked Menard, feeling a sick drop in his gut.

"Not likely," McNally stated flatly. "Anarchists running an investment consortium? Seems odd to me."

Kewitt again: "Embeddeds."

A number of things slid into place in Menard's head in that moment. He wasn't sure what, or how, but he had that prickling feeling that came when an idea was materializing. Along with the bone chill. *Am I close, Lord?* "Embeddeds...."

McNally glanced from his CPO to the Chor Episcopos and back again. "Embeddeds?"

Menard waved him off. *Think, think*. The Embedded Hypothesis was the least credible of the nonlunatic theories about xenics. In fact, a lot of people considered it the reverse, the most credible of the lunatic theories.

But Embeddeds would care about an insurance scam. And Embeddeds might have some reason to build a shipyard.

"Chor Episcopos," said McNally. "I'm sorry, sir, but this may affect my ship. What's an Embedded?"

"It's an extreme form of Internalism. Not academically significant, nor much in fashion among serious thinkers of my generation." Menard laughed. "I strongly doubt it myself, but the Embedded Hypothesis might account for more of the facts than any other xenic theory. Though truth be told, I find it more likely the Black Flag is behind all this."

"Extreme Internalism? Like my rockships, but more so?"

Kewitt nodded. "Yes, sir."

"He's right, as far as it goes." Menard stood, found his way to the galley section tucked behind the massive coffee machine, and began looking for a steak of his own. He called out over his shoulder: "Basically, the idea is that the xenics are among us, but indistinguishable from human beings. They might even be in positions of authority and trust, guiding our affairs to their own ends. Not just moving among our culture, but sitting at our desks, wearing our clothes. Possibly giving our orders."

McNally snorted. "Respectfully sir, that's ridiculous. Too many medical checks, for one."

"Precisely. Consider this: We have hundreds of worlds' worth of parallel evolution to analyze. There's only so many morphologies to go around. Goodness, there's only so many *biochemistries* to go around, at least in an oxygen–nitrogen atmosphere with a carbon-based molecular ecology. Even so, there's never been a genetic structure close enough to Earth-normal to fool even the most casual analysis. No Embedded xenic would ever make it through any role more complicated than farming on a newly opened world. And that only seen from a distance, probably."

"So where's the nonlunatic part begin?"

Menard set his steak in the cooker, punched a few buttons, then turned to lean on the corner of the big brass coffee machine. "Well, Ken, there isn't a nonlunatic part. Unless you're willing to believe in mimics or doppelgangers or some kind of brain-eating virus. For which there has never been any evidence."

"Skipper keeps a rock watch," said Kewitt with a smile.

"Lots of people believe in lots of things," McNally acknowledged, "but that one's just silly on the face of it."

"I agree, Lieutenant. But still, I'd like to talk to Ser

Micah Albrecht over there in *Jenny's Little Pearl*. He set off a nest of something. If nothing else, there's a lot of money unaccounted for in this system. Someone built that shipyard for some reason." He paused. "Tell me, Lieutenant, can you get me to Ser Albrecht's destination any faster?"

"Yes," said McNally. "I could stuff you into a fast packet and shoot you off. That would violate my orders to protect and secure you, and probably contravene your own instructions as well. You'd be completely vulnerable in transit, and *St. Gaatha* hours behind you once you arrived. And you wouldn't enjoy the trip one bit, I assure you."

"I'll have the angel. I don't think it would let me go alone even if I wanted to."

McNally chewed the last of his steak. "There is that."

#

Albrecht: Halfsummer Solar Space, The Necklace
Ignoring the burning pain in his left wrist—the bandage and med-nano goop didn't seem to be coping very well so far with newt saliva or whatever had gotten into him—Albrecht nuked up four kilos of that horrible chicken fried rice from the galley. There didn't seem to be any suitable containers, so he tore a cushion off the number three crew station in the bridge and piled the steaming mess into the cover. "Boat, is the newt at the fore or aft end of the passage?"

"It is currently at the aft end."

"Moving around or what?"

"It is currently stationary."

Albrecht had flooded the passage with a decimeter of water a few hours earlier. It seemed to be the kindest thing to do, since the newt was an amphibian and he wasn't trying to kill it at the moment.

"Cycle the forward hatch to that passage on my say-so. *Don't* leave it open." Albrecht didn't want to find out the hard way how fast the damned thing could move. Steaming mess of food in the upholstery in his hand, Albrecht stood just outside the entrance to the portside passage. "Three, two, one, go!" The hatch slid open with a hiss, and Albrecht dumped the steaming rice over the coaming onto the floor beyond. "Close it already!" he shouted as a hundred kilos of enraged newt scuttled down the twenty-meter passageway toward him.

The thump echoed through the bulkhead.

He slid into the command station and called up a camera view of the newt's passageway. It was investigating the rice. "Best I can do for you, buddy," Albrecht told the image, then set the main screen back to tracking his trackers.

Petrograd still trailed him, keeping about a quarter light-second of separation. The new bogie, which his boat's systems wanted to call *St. Gaatha*, would overhaul him a few hours after he hit The Necklace. Albrecht had laid in a course for Shorty's Surprise, a medium-sized port inside The Necklace. He wondered how lost he could get in there.

Pearl also helpfully informed him of a new arrival to Halfsummer, something military and uninterested in advertising its identity that had a forty-one percent probability of making Shorty's Surprise within eight hours of his own arrival.

"Where the hell are all these people coming from?"

While he was looking at the pitifully thin data on the new bogie, he noticed he had mail as well.

#

To: Micah Albrecht/Jenny's Little Pearl/In Transit
Fr: Lt. Alma Gorova/Public Safety/

Gryphon Landing/Halfsummer
Re: Insurance Fraud
Ser Albrecht—

I would take it as a great personal favor if, in the time before one or another of your enemies finally succeeds in killing you and destroying the boat you have commandeered, you might take a few moments and write me a note outlining what you have learned about *Jenny's Diamond Bright* and such fraud issues as you may have acquired firsthand knowledge of. While we are both clear on your attitudes toward law enforcement in particular and authority in general, your information may prove invaluable toward saving the lives of other spacers not so atavistically inclined as yourself. Consider it a public service.

Remain in health, so long as you are able.

—Lt. Gorova

#

Such a humorist the watch commander was. Albrecht cursed under his breath for a while, offered up a vain prayer, then wrote out an explanation of his experiences to that point. All he wanted to do was leave—he didn't give a damn about the Black Flag, insurance, the Navy, or anything else. He just wanted out.

He made that very clear in his note, then stored it on a hotkey to squirt back dirtside in case things got terminally interesting before he made port at Shorty's Surprise.

#

Albrecht managed to feed the newt twice more over the next day and half. He had a feeling he might want its help later. The creature seemed to be less enthusiastic about charging the hatch each time he opened it, though the smell could have stunned an AI. Albrecht preferred to ascribe the hanging back to low animal cunning rather than any instinct to be tamed for hand-feeding. He'd considered turning the gravimetrics off to confuse it. The repairs he'd been able to make were a bit dodgy, and the animal was by nature a swimmer anyway and thus presumably equipped to cope with moving in three dimensions, so he figured he was best off leaving well enough alone.

In the idle hours of transit he caught up on his sleep and established that yes, the military newcomer would almost certainly be closing vectors with him in the belt. He still had no idea who the hell that was. Exploring *Pearl* further in his spare time, he found some of the smuggling compartments, which conveniently yielded to his codelock key. Albrecht suddenly didn't have money problems any more, though he had shit all to spend it on.

After he'd counted out a few thousand credits, he tried tapping into the systemwide nöosphere. Dirtside newsfeeds were more attenuated this far out, but it looked like the Imperial Resident had clamped down on the holy heck he'd unleashed back in Gryphon Landing. There was one city he probably shouldn't expect to ever return to.

Oddly, though Albrecht had seen his own name in the 'casts, no one had ever identified his boat. He tried to decide whether that was good for him or bad for him. Like everything else lately, the whole business was a bit of a toss-up.

By the time he made The Necklace and Shorty's local

space, he was heartily sick of *Jenny D*, Halfsummer, the newt, the Navy, the Church, and pretty much everything and everyone else in the universe not named Micah Albrecht.

#

It was, he had to admit, a sight to behold. Albrecht wasn't really an aficionado of belt industrial complexes. He was a c-spacer, not a local yokel, and his crew time had been aboard liners and high-end freighters that moved station-to-station. Still, he'd seen enough adventure virteos set among rough-and-tumble belt miners and their hard-bitten crews to have some notion of what a belt port was supposed to look like.

The Necklace, and Shorty's Surprise, did not disappoint.

For one, The Necklace had an unusually high albedo. That was what made it visible from Halfsummer's nights. Up close the belt glittered like a sky full of diamonds. Which, in a sense, it was—a significant proportion of ice chunks and a high concentration of metallic salts and crystals in the rocky bodies created the bright reflections of light from the primary, and also made The Necklace a rich environment for mining.

The individual rocks and snowballs of The Necklace didn't tumble and shift, like asteroid belts always seemed to do in the virteos. Rather, they were strung along in a staggered line, resembling nothing so much as a poorly maintained gas giant ring system. Shorty's Surprise sat embedded in this glittering arc of sky like a jewelry mount waiting for just the right gem cut to come along.

The core of the mount was a large chunk of hardware—maybe an old ice cracking plant?—to which three rather substantial rocks had been tethered and spun up to rotation. That would produce a useful illusion of gravity via centripetal force, but not normal to the intended gravity plane of the original structure. And of course, the axis of rotation would be in microgravity.

That was a lot of trouble to go to for some g-force, given the prevalence of gravimetrics, but the whole business made Shorty's Surprise damned hard to get into in a hurry, Albrecht figured. Also made it less vulnerable to power failures. All that rotation was better than armor, assuming the bad guys didn't just settle for blowing the whole thing up. Cut down on the armed raids, at any rate, he'd bet.

He couldn't quite tell what the station had been made from because it had been built out, ramified, turned into something very unlike the crisp, clean lines he was used to seeing in space operations areas—all the work apparently done by crazy people. As the rocks turned on the ends of their tethers, Albrecht could see they were covered with huge, obscene carvings. Amid the massive, distorted genitalia and assorted protest symbols was a collection of stone buildings, bubble shelters, gutted rock hoppers, a scattering of engine mounts—to manage gyroscopic precession?—and supply dumps, all tethered down to keep it from flying off into space.

The cables connecting the rocks to the core were clear and unobstructed, either out of some rudimentary notion of safety, or perhaps as a transitway. The core itself was a jumble of metal sculptures—he spotted a giant, eyeless face spinning past, lips curled in disdain, nostrils flared wide—boat hulls welded or tethered into place, biofactory pods and glowing spots where something arced free with a purple-blue glow he wouldn't care to be any closer to.

It was a station as designed by the artistic and the insane. It was junk and movement and life, and even to Albrecht's prosaic and battered soul, an obvious shout against the cold darkness of life in hard vacuum. It was also a maintenance nightmare and a cold metal deathtrap that wouldn't pass a restaurant health inspection.

"Boat, what's our approach?"

"System info says under local control. There is no standard approach documented."

Uh huh. "Well, would you please patch me in to localspace approach control?"

"Of course," said *Pearl*. "Stand by."

A few moments later a rough female voice crackled through the bridge. No video or virteo feed, of course. "Shorty's. Whaddayawan'?"

"*Jenny's Little Pearl* requesting approach vector and docking instructions."

There was snort. Then: "You must be new here." She launched into what was obviously a prepared speech. "Come in dead slow, don't hit nothing. Park it off the celestial north axis and walk in. No weapons. Someone will shake you down at the airlock. They prolly won't be gentle."

"Uh... thank you, Shorty's."

"Whaddeva."

Albrecht had always worked major ports. The flight instructions here represented a fairly unique traffic control policy, in his experience. On the other hand, a station the size of Shorty's Surprise didn't come with the sort of entrenched bureaucracy that infested the class I and II ports *Princess Janivera* had called at. He cycled his main screen through the closing vectors on his two pursuing bogies... six point one hours for the God squad, and seven point eight hours for the stealthy combat unit. Hammer and anvil. With *Novy Petrograd* nearby to document the destruction. He wondered how mad the station administrators at Shorty's Surprise would be at him for bringing in that kind of trouble.

With any luck, he'd be long gone before either of

the bad guys got here.

Albrecht cycled his screen back to approach view, and went in on instruments rather than the usual port control. Dead slow was dead slow. Given the sheer amount of junk tethered to or orbiting Shorty's Surprise, and that three-balled bola whirling demonically just beneath his line of travel, that was a fine speed for his peace of mind.

He didn't hit nothing, either. Or at least *Pearl*'s autopilot systems didn't. Albrecht found a place to park *Pearl*, tucked in fairly close to a derelict gasbag apparently long retired from outer system towing runs. The gasbag seemed to be stationkeeping with respect to Shorty's Surprise via an odd assortment of strapped-on thrusters, as were the rather numerous collections of rock tugs, orbit hoppers, runabouts, broom sticks, and jack-built scooters parked in a rough array around Shorty's axis of rotation. Albrecht set *Pearl* up to keep station with respect to the gasbag, with breakaway orders to go to a ten-thousand-meter standoff if the immediate area got violent or junky, either one.

All he had to do now was walk in. Which was to say, take a short, slow, controlled excursion from *Pearl*'s airlock through the crap-filled vacuum of immediate localspace to the lock at the celestial north end of Shorty's axis of rotation. Easy enough.

Then he realized his problem. The main airlock was off the portside passage. The spacesuit locker was off the portside passage. The portside passage was currently occupied by a hundred kilos of pissed-off Halfsummer newt.

"Damn, damn, damn," shouted Albrecht at the empty, uncaring bridge of his little boat.

#

Ten minutes later he'd worked it out. A couple of kilos

of that horrid chicken fried rice in the *aft* cross-passage, in front of the engineering section. Then have *Pearl* open the connecting hatch. The newt would go in to feed, he'd slip through the portside passage into the suit locker and on to the airlock.

Simple enough. All he had to do was preprogram the sequence of his movements about the boat into *Pearl*'s systems. Albrecht figured on taking the codelock key with him, as well as a pile of those credits he'd stumbled over, while securing all the boards and boat systems against unexpected visitors. Assuming they survived the newt, they still wouldn't be able to do so much as get a hatch opened without the key.

He decided to leave the aft cross-passage open to the portside passage. When he needed to get back, he'd deal with the newt, probably by having *Pearl* shift hatches 'til the newt moved on somewhere else.

No point in not giving it the run of the ship, at least in the areas where any intruders were likely to come in. There wasn't much he could do if the bad guys decided to cut through the hull.

He flexed his aching wrist and wished whoever came after him the joy of the chase. Then Albrecht finished setting his instructions into the systems, fired off his letter to Public Safety Lieutenant Alma Gorova, primed the lockdown routines, and went about luring the newt out of his way.

#

"How much can one lizard piss?" Albrecht grumbled, wading through the water toward the airlock. The newt thumped against the closed hatch from the aft cross-passage, trying to get back to its erstwhile home. His nose was being assaulted by a rank, swampy odor that made his eyes water. He didn't want to think about what this stuff was doing to his boots.

No wonder the watermen of Gryphon landing were such an ill-tempered bunch of piss-takers. If this was what their canals and marshes smelled like, they could hardly be anything else. Not with spending their days out there breathing this god-awful crud.

He cycled open the suit locker. All the repair work he had done before he'd been chased out of Halfsummer orbit by *Petrograd* meant that Albrecht had experienced a good opportunity to work with the inventory. He'd actually managed to cobble together an engineering hardsuit that more or less fit him—the closest thing to combat armor a civilian could legally use. Albrecht unclipped the welder and power feed attachments currently in place on the suit arms. He figured whoever did the shakedowns at Shorty's front door would consider them weapons, regardless of the manufacturer's intended use.

He strapped in to the suit while still standing ankle-deep in the mucky water in the passageway. That meant his suit liner became wet, being infiltrated with that same hideous smell. Albrecht was not very pleased with life by the time he squeezed himself into the airlock.

Time to go for a walk.

#

Golliwog: Halfsummer Solar Space, In transit
They flew wrapped in an inner darkness that mimicked the world outside, breathing stale air and the edge of one another's sweat. Yee's boat, nameless and unregistered, was stealthy across all systems Golliwog could analyze, stripped to the essentials except for a few operational flourishes. Much of the hull was transparent to visible light—inbound only, based on what he had seen in the boat deck—but still the interior was quite shadowed. Golliwog presumed that this avoided light leakage through potential hull flaws, but more to the point the

low illumination kept the occupants extremely focused on their surroundings.

It was sort of like being projected through space in a reasonably comfortable chair.

Ahead of them The Necklace gleamed, a bright spill of water braiding its way through space. Golliwog knew that Halfsummer's belt was considered beautiful, but his aesthetic criteria had always been largely functional. Like this boat, for example. If something cut well, without wasted material or motion, it was elegant. Even so there was something moving about the sight, that spoke to the human soul buried somewhere beneath all the gene grafts and surgeries and biomechanical enhancements that made him the bione Golliwog instead of one of Eve's grandchildren.

Or perhaps great-grandchildren?

The traitor voice that was slowly unfolding in his mind wondered whether the feeling created by this view was what Holy Communion tasted like.

Holy or not, Yee's little vessel was the finest boat he'd ever flown. Golliwog felt the sheer joy of the overpowered drives reacting to his touch. Nothing that moved had unlimited acceleration—no matter how efficiently the hydrogen conversion process was tuned, physics and fuel capacity set limits—but Yee's dark, illegal little craft was as close as he'd ever come to that experience.

"We're going to miss him by about an hour," Yee muttered. She was watching a low-lux screen that plotted their intercept. "I expected to do better than this."

Golliwog heard the reproof in her voice. "It flies, ma'am. And quite quickly. But that's all it does." Nothing beyond the possible.

"Not your error, Golliwog. We could perhaps have optimized a launch curve from *Hinton*, but I didn't assess the need quickly enough. Captain Hawking is worthless."

"Ma'am." He didn't need to comment further on Naval politics. Golliwog was perfectly aware that he existed on the sufferance of his late training partners, the various Examining Boards, and distant committees of men and women much like both Yee and Hawking.

"I've been going through the files on our destination. Shorty's Surprise. Typical belter crap."

His scalp prickled. Yee rarely used profanity.

She continued: "We could make a hard entry, but that would not serve our purposes. They have a fairly crude protocol, which we can walk through. I am an information smuggler, you are my muscle. I will make sure to carry sufficient credits in hardmoney to get us past the door wardens. Stick to your class three armament, but don't argue if they take anything away from you."

"Ma'am, yes ma'am."

"Inside… we want to speak to Ser Albrecht privately, at some length. We do not wish to terminate him unless he seems to be breaking free of our control in some irrevocable manner. Are we in agreement?"

"Ma'am, yes ma'am." Golliwog wondered where she had gone while he was waiting in the boat bay, what Spinks had told her or what comm signal Yee had received that now made her so furiously, dangerously tense. "Ma'am?"

"Yes?"

"What do I do if something happens to you?" *Free, walk free*, said the voice inside his head. *Don't let them strap you down and study whatever's wrong with your mind in c-space*.

She laughed. It was an edgy sound, buzzed, full of hormones and little knives. "Anything that happens to me will have to finish happening to you first, Golliwog."

"Ma'am, yes ma'am."

He concentrated on flying. Golliwog found himself sincerely hoping that Captain Hawking had managed to extract some additional acceleration out of *Dmitri Hinton*. He wasn't feeling very confident in the face of Yee's obvious stress.

#

Menard: Halfsummer Solar Space, In transit

McNally had not been jesting about Menard finding the experience unenjoyable. Menard wondered whether he could hold his breath for the next several hours. Doubtless the angel could.

The two of them lay close together, stretched out flat, side by side in a simple, enclosed tube. Menard wore a skinsuit, with softbubble helmet and a ninety-minute bottle stowed somewhere just above his head. The angel still wore its red leather armor, which strongly implied the blessèd thing was vacuum-rated.

Their fast packet was just that—a fast packet. A single h-q conversion engine, just enough gravimetrics to keep the inside of the tube from being filled with passenger jelly upon maneuvering, and some little idiot AI pilot. Building small was expensive. Menard shuddered to think what this thing cost—the equivalent of a significant portion of *St. Gaatha*'s entire construction budget, he'd wager.

The same peculiar math that required the fast courier to be massive in order to optimize the process of entering and emerging from c-transition worked against the ship in realspace. A couple of equation values flipped back to what Einstein or even Newton might have understood. Once that happened, down in normal space *St. Gaatha* was a big, slow chunk of metal being pushed around on an exhaust column.

Hence fast packets. When something, or someone,

had to get somewhere without delay. C-transitions simply weren't possible too deep within gravity wells. Otherwise the Church Militant vessel could have just skipped like a stone across the Halfsummer system. *That* was a piece of math and engineering that had eluded the hopeful for over a thousand years.

So here he was, scooting across too many light-seconds' distance stuffed in a pipe with a stone killer committed to the glory of God.

This was why God had given man prayer. As a comfort in times of trial.

"Be mindful, O Lord," the Chor Episcopos began, then wondered why he was muttering. This was an angel next to him, crowded up against him. Surely it did not resent prayer. At least his knees did not burn, folded in here. He addressed himself to God: "Mindful of those who travel by land, by sea, by air, and by space; of the old and young, the sick, the suffering, the sorrowing, the afflicted, the captives, the needy, and the poor; and upon them all send forth Thy mercies, for Thou art the Giver of all good things."

From there he slid into silent meditation, considering the life of St. Niphon as that venerable's earthly works and place in Heaven applied to one frightened priest sliding through vacuum in the company of terror, bound for what might be the greatest discovery of his age. Hope, and pride, were a spark beneath his fear and worry.

#

Albrecht: Halfsummer Solar Space, The Necklace, Shorty's Surprise

He'd be damned if he understood how they got anything done out here. The immediate localspace around the station was a fog of dust, ice crystals, loose tools, stray scrap. He even saw a mummified cat drift by as his engineering hardsuit's tiny attitude jets eased Albrecht toward the airlock at the top of the axis of Shorty's Surprise.

The perspective was gut-wrenching. Shorty's balls spun around three hundred meters or so below his line of travel with a velocity of about eighty or ninety meters per second along their outer edge—making their rotation about once every forty-five seconds. That was naked-eye fast, especially with those rockballs massing so many tons. In space, naked-eye fast generally meant fatally fast. Like climbing into the Empire's largest coffee grinder.

The cloud of junk moved too, traveling through The Necklace with Shorty's Surprise, and swirling in some vague convection of gravitational pull and constant tiny collisions. It occurred to Albrecht to wonder why the orbiting crap didn't just head out of the little system. Did they actually herd this stuff back into place?

The whole setup was frightening.

The old ice cracking plant rotated with alarming velocity as well, though being at the core of the little dynamic system it didn't have quite the gut-blurring effect of the tethered rockballs, not as far as Albrecht's sense of well-being was concerned. A huge shaft rose out of the central core. The conning module from some long-vanished rock tug perched at the tip, gimbaled and counterrotating to provide a modicum of sanity for the approaching traveler.

It was lit up, with "Do Not Enter" spelled out in seven alphabetic languages, two sets of ideograms, a script he didn't recognize, and Imperial Standard Safety Glyphs. He presumed that was the entry. The shakedown point.

Albrecht landed the hardsuit outside a hatch about four meters wide by three tall—equipment lock, then, but not big enough for boats—immediately beneath the large, lit-up glyph panels. He looked around for a keypad to buzz in. Nothing. He considered calling on Shorty's frequency, but given the enthusiasm with which his last call had been met, Albrecht wasn't sure that game was worth the oxygen candle.

Surely they were watching him. As junky and weird as this setup was, it was also a damned good fishtrap for wayward bandits—both a spacer and his vessel could fail to return from here quite easily. Most likely neither would ever be missed if they hadn't logged a good flight plan somewhere.

He settled for powering his right glove to max output and pounding on the lock panels. If the intermediate chamber was under pressure, that ought to echo pretty well within. He felt sort of like the newt, hurling itself against the hatches of *Jenny's Little Pearl*.

Then the doors slid back in a widening rhombus. He stepped forward into the light where three burly gentlemen in skinsuits awaited him.

#

The shakedown wasn't so bad. The gleesome threesome—close relatives, possibly clones or some such, and, judging from their size and muscle development, engineered far past human norms of power and strength—popped the seals on his hardsuit. None too brutally they skinned Albrecht out of it, patted him down for blades, slugthrowers, and energy weapons, impounded half his cash, and shoved him out the other side of the lock. The side with air pressure.

One of the monsters had trailed after him, proffering a receipt for the cash and the hardsuit. Albrecht took it. "Thanks."

"Drink," rumbled his minder. The man—Albrecht thought he was a man—had a voice that practically possessed its own plate tectonics. It matched his muscle grafts and subcutaneous armor.

Albrecht wasn't sure whether that was a question, a suggestion, or an order, so he replied, "Lead the way." It was a good bet that if he were looking for crew to hire, they'd be wherever the booze was.

The interior of Shorty's Surprise was every bit as bizarre as the exterior. Whatever the central body had originally been, that had involved a series of tall pressure vessels. These were now in the fractional-g zone near the axis of rotation, something down around .1 or maybe even lower. The locals had taken advantage of the situation to intercut the old thick-walled cylinders with balconies, walkways, ladders, and every kind of dwelling or storage space human ingenuity could bring to bear out of a good-sized orbital scrap yard and a pressurized, low-gee environment. People walked, worked, laughed, screamed, fucked, flew all around Albrecht. The air smelled of a hundred scents, everything from the strange plastic odor of reentry-rated paint to good old-fashioned sweat to cooking with spices he couldn't have named for a million credits but still made his mouth water.

And there were children everywhere. Scampering, climbing, leaping across open spaces like wriggling, wingless birds. Human enough—he didn't see muties or any evidence of bione surgeries—and every shade of melanin in the gene pool, all mixed together in one extended, screaming mass woven in and around the mélange of commerce and architecture in which they lived.

Albrecht suddenly wondered why he'd never liked children. These people weren't dregs, he realized. They were a breeding ground, hurtling across empty space toward some destination he couldn't know, just as their children leaped unheeded into open air. He continued to muse as his minder led him along an intestinally complex path through several of the tall caverns, in and out of fogs of cuisine and different varieties of labor, before stopping in front of a storefront that appeared to be made of actual wood—that a luxury more rare than gemstones out in the Deep Dark, he knew.

"Here," the big man rumbled.

"Thanks," said Albrecht, and stepped inside.

Anybody who watched virteos knew what a belt miners' bar looked like. Sort of a spacegoing version of The Newt Trap back at Gryphon Landing—grubby, crowded, filled with souvenirs and detritus of sweaty men and women laboring in honest toil. This wasn't any such thing. This was… a bubble of beauty inside the postindustrial chaos teeming around it.

Everything wall-like was also a wooden floor, arrayed in a rough dodecahedron. This close to the center of Shorty's Surprise, there was no real sense of "down." Brass rails served as rungs and handholds, and as Albrecht looked he realized the floor had been laid in long, thin sections secured with brass studs or nails.

It really was a work of art.

The bar proper was a smaller dodecahedron at the center of the room, connected by brass pipework positioned normal to the axis-of-spin. That would carry utility feeds, of course. The center dodecahedron had folding panels, so that it had been opened up in a sort of underlit latticework inside of which several people cooked, poured, and otherwise tended bar.

The patrons were clustered around the outer rim of the room, hooked on to the ladders and railing, some using little portable tables to secure their drinks. A few people moved in groups of two or three in the open space between the englobing floor and the central bar—microgravity dancing, Albrecht realized.

"This is what you dream here, isn't it?" he

whispered.

"Dreams are good," rumbled the minder, bursting into intelligible speech somewhat to Albrecht's surprise. "Sit here by the wall. I'll get drinks."

Albrecht sat. He looked. He wondered what it meant to make a home in Shorty's Surprise. Obviously people were born, lived, and died here. It was a sort of fishtrap, all right, but a fishtrap for the future as much as for the past. Offense, not defense, for a culture Albrecht had never had much connection with.

It was the first place in the entire Halfsummer system where he'd felt welcome. Or at least comfortable.

The minder came back, two low-gee drink bulbs swinging from one paw. "Here."

"Thank you," said Albrecht. He looked it over. Unlabeled.

His host grinned, a somewhat alarming sight given the cracked ceramics that passed for teeth in his mouth. "Sugar water. You've got trouble coming, don't need to be drunk."

"Excuse me?"

"We watch the newsfeeds." He leaned forward. "*Carefully*. And your boat. We know your boat. You got two kinds of problems chasing you, plus Ballbuster Bourne floating around out there somewhere keeping the box scores."

"Then you know about the Writ of Attainder," Albrecht said.

The minder shrugged.

"Who are the other guys?"

"Naval Oversight."

Albrecht choked on his sugar water, spraying a cloud of the stuff. Spitting fluid in low gee was damned near a cardinal sin for a spacer, but his host just swatted it away. "They're... they're worse than the fucking Church...."

Albrecht had urgent need of a head call, given how his gut had just begun gurgling.

"Two problems, no waiting." The big man grinned again. "But maybe you're the person to carry some problems away."

"You guys allergic to *Jenny D* too? They didn't like her much along the water docks back in Gryphon Landing."

"You might say that."

"Can I ask your name?"

The minder mulled that over for a moment. "Call me Dillon."

"Thank you," said Albrecht. "Look, Dillon. I just came here looking for crew, people that might want to ship out. Go claim *Jenny D* from a cold orbit, if she's still c-worthy, and leave. I didn't expect to find a… a… city here."

"No." Dillon's eyes narrowed. "Who does? We're scum. Pirates. Fools. Ask anyone. The Empire, it's for rich people who walk on dirt, fly between the stars in pretty plastic ships. We're just who we are."

"People." Albrecht had never really thought about that, what it meant to be *from* a place like The Necklace. "Making, living, dying." He stopped. "Killing, too."

"Black Flag? That's the anger of people like us. Striking a blow against the past. This…" One huge hand swept to include the bar, and possibly all of Shorty's Surprise beyond. "This is the future of people like us. I hope you see the difference." Dillon locked gazes with him. "You part of our anger, Micah Albrecht, or part of our future?"

Around them, the bar had fallen silent. Albrecht was aware of several dozen pairs of eyes watching him. This question was important. Whether he ever got back to *Pearl*, whether he ever found *Jenny D*, might hang on his answer. And how many of the people in here were Black Flag cell members? The minder had all but said Black Flag was powerful here.

It was Micah Albrecht who hung on the answer, he realized. Who he was, what he stood for.

"What am I signing up for?" he finally asked, softly.

The answer was quick, brusque: "You tell me." Testing.

He thought that over carefully. These people, hiding out here in the dark, they were building. Not destroying. The violent opportunism of the Black Flag hadn't created this place. And Albrecht wasn't a violent man either. "I... I'm not made for anger."

"Fair enough. But mark this. Anger's been made aplenty for you. There's angry people following you out there. Black Flag has your name, too."

"That's as it may be. I just want to get on with life."

"So you choose the future?"

Albrecht took a deep breath. "Yes."

Dillon grinned, more broadly than before. "Good. In that case, allow me to show you the past."

Everyone in the bar around them began moving with rapid, coordinated purpose.

#

Golliwog: Halfsummer Solar Space, The Necklace, Shorty's Surprise

"These people need to be exterminated," Yee muttered on their suit band. "For the sake of public health and safety."

Golliwog steered his own skinsuit toward the garish entrance. It was, he had to admit, so unlike the localspace environment around Powell Station that he wondered if this were a setup. A graduation exercise. Surely no one could build such an improbable installation as Shorty's Surprise? The architecture was bizarre, the maintenance nonexistent. Even the name was ridiculous.

And this fog of garbage and scrap and water ice. You could lose anything in it.

Including, he realized, fog. Golliwog suddenly wondered how much nanotrace there was around him. The glittering fog of high-end defensive tech would be utterly anonymous in this environment. *Something* had to be maintaining the cohesion of the junk cloud—most of it would have dispersed on its own, scattered by the angular momentum of this little system. The localspace cloud made rapid maneuvering challenging, too. He realized that this selfsame chaotic nonsense might in fact be quite a good defense. Especially if one was chronically underfunded and short on supplies.

He had to admit, they had a certain style.

As Yee reached the lock just ahead of him, one of the locals dropped down from the shadowed space behind the overlit glyphs. Yee pushed off from the decklip of the lock, putting space between her and the intruder. It took Golliwog a few precious seconds to realize what had set the doctor so suddenly in motion.

The local wasn't wearing a suit.

He was a freak, too. Golliwog knew from freaks, given the circumstances of his own short life. This one was three meters tall, lanky as a sipping straw, with dead white skin, red body armor, and a red cross tattooed on his forehead.

And apparently capable of standing around in hard vacuum. Not much frightened Golliwog, but *that* scared him.

Yee's voice crackled in his helmet, tight, controlled. "Microthin skinsuit. Fucker's showing off."

The fear slumped through Golliwog's guts, already

turning into a hot ball of anger, when the red-and-white bastard spread sparkling gossamer wings and went after Dr. Yee.

Golliwog amped up his own systems, going into full offensive mode, and shot his skinsuit on an intercept course with the enemy's most probable vector.

"Angel!" Yee shouted, starfishing her body to meet her attacker.

Angel? He wasn't sure how Yee knew their opponent's name, but it didn't matter. What mattered was that this Angel would have several precious seconds to tear at Yee before Golliwog could close.

But then, Dr. Yee was a Marine pathfinder.

Golliwog opened a carrier signal from the chips inside his head, to see whether there were any Naval-grade nano spread around him. There was a flashing ripple in the fog, but he didn't get the correct countersigns. His open weapons underneath his skinsuit, Golliwog snatched at likely-looking junk as he hurtled toward the combatants.

Angel came at Yee hands forward, wings wide, like red vengeance. Yee's open-limbed posture let her fold around Angel's left hand as soon as he caught her. Golliwog saw that blow land, saw the shock ripple through Yee's skinsuit, but still she used Angel's arm as a lever, twisting the hand and forearm against the natural range of motion of the elbow to give her control of his actions and effectively neutralize his advantage of velocity.

That move would have disabled any ordinary human who didn't get free in time. Angel didn't bother to twist free, but his arm didn't break backward either. Yee simply ran out of range-of-travel, her body absorbing another shock as she stopped unexpectedly.

She held her grip on Angel's wrist, though.

Golliwog closed then, his original course calculation being only a few percentage points in error. He swung the ice-covered strip of metal in his left hand, aiming through the gossamer wing toward the red-clad back, even as his right landed for a grip on Angel's flank—in low-gee combat, a blow was close to meaningless if the combatant was not also anchored to the opponent's body.

But the wing, almost illusory to the eye, slowed the swing of Golliwog's right hand to a crawl, then a stop. He felt a fire in his nerves, followed by a frightening dullness, as both biological and enhanced circuits shorted out.

Golliwog's right hand landed above Angel's hip in that moment, and he converted his momentum to a sort of hug, trying to duck his head and upper torso beneath the sweep of the wings, aiming for the lower back.

Angel's left leg folded upward in reverse—a skeletal impossibility in Golliwog's considerable experience—sweeping a foot into the line of travel of his chest. Golliwog rolled close into this move, trying to take the blow on his side instead of his sternum, even as he heard Yee broadcast a startled grunt and saw a spray of icing blood gleaming in the light from the station's glyphs.

The backward kick connected with a crack of Golliwog's carbonmesh-reinforced ribs. But he was closed in now, close, hugging Angel's right leg with his deadening left arm. Golliwog flipped another metal strip into his right hand and stabbed upward into Angel's groin. Between the legs, he saw Yee land a two-legged kick on Angel's face.

Someone short and chubby in a skinsuit and softbubble helmet swam across Golliwog's line of site, arms waving madly. Angel went limp, releasing Yee. Golliwog took that moment to drive his metal into the groin one more time—no one had released *him*. Even as the blow landed, Yee's voice crackled in his helmet, wavering and shrill as he'd ever heard it: "Stand down, Golliwog."

Despite the order, Golliwog held his follow-through, making sure Angel felt it. No point in breaking his training now. Was that rebellion or loyalty? Crimson ice trailed from Yee's suit, punctuation to both emotions.

#

Menard: Halfsummer Solar Space, The Necklace, Shorty's Surprise

"By the bones of Saint Tikhon!" Menard shouted. This was a disaster. The blesséd angel had started a fight it couldn't finish. That alone was astonishing.

Who *were* these people?

The three combatants circled warily. The smaller of the two strange fighters was in a bad way, he could see, but there was something wrong with the angel as well. The… wide… stranger seemed to have trouble controlling his movements.

The Chor Episcopos took a deep breath, prayed for wisdom, then spread his arms wide. The cross stenciled on the breast of his skinsuit should make his status clear enough. That they had stopped fighting told him these newcomers weren't Black Flag or random criminals—those sorts wouldn't have bothered to break off until they'd prevailed or been thoroughly beaten. Which in space tended to be an especially final result.

The particulate fog around him glittered in a new pattern, flashing light and dark as if something invisible rippled through it. He didn't know what that activity meant, but it didn't seem good. Progressing with deliberate movements borne of both caution and clumsiness—he was suit-trained and vacuum-rated, but Menard would never have expert's comfort in microgravity—he made his way to the huge airlock.

There was no comm plate that he could find there. Menard patted the outer shell of the station, looking among the welded and hammered artwork of tortured faces and exploding suns for a control panel access. He had no success, but as he searched, the lock slid open, four sections retracting at shallow angles to one another in a bright diamond of light.

One very large man stood there anchored to the deck, backlit to an angular silhouette, carrying a very large weapon. Menard turned to look at the angel and its erstwhile combatants. The silver-bright ripples in the fog had thickened around them while his attention was focused on the hatch.

All three were still.

The very large man waved Menard into the lock. As he drifted inside, a group of hard-suited flyers appeared out of the junk cloud—they must have exited another lock nearby. His last sight of the battle scene was a net being fired toward the angel.

The very large man snapped the Chor Episcopos's helmet off as soon as there was sufficient ambient pressure in the lock chamber. His own followed a moment later, releasing a cloud of red hair that fuzzed out in the microgravity. The very large weapon remained poised at the ready, though, he noticed. It was a ballspitter—personnel suppression at its finest, not intended to be fatal. Though this particular ballspitter was the biggest such device Menard had ever seen.

"It is that you have one minute to be telling me what you are of doing here," his captor said in a thick Franco-Minionese accent.

She was a woman, Menard realized. Another tailored freak like the fighter outside. What God's people did to their own bodies was both a sin and a tragedy. Right here, right now, his only leverage was to stand on his position. "I am the Honorable Reverend Chor Episcopos Jonah Menard. I am here to serve a Writ of Attainder against Micah Albrecht and *Jenny's Little Pearl*."

"And it is for this reason your beast she jumped upon strangers? The forty-five seconds, Chor Episcopos."

"I beg forgiveness. My, ah, beast, is an angel, a servant of the Patriarchy." He could not bear false witness, sadly enough in this case where it might have been convenient. Menard felt a fleeting longing for McNally's creative approach to ethics and regulations. "It judged danger to my person and my mission from the strangers. I am not certain why."

The very large woman cocked her head for a moment, listening. Then: "What is it the building number of the Security Directorate of the Personnel Bureau? My pardon, of the Personnel Bureau of the Directorate?"

"Three seventeen," blurted Menard, surprised at the question. That was Prime See detail, not common conversational fodder out here in the fields of Empire. Trivia, to be sure, and a clever way of checking his claim, but an odd thing for these people to know.

Her head cocked a moment more. "To be congratulated. You are living. You word for bond on the others?"

"Others? I don't know the two who fought the angel."

"We judge the angel is to have won, so the others they are the prisoners of you."

"*Who* are they?"

"How you say… hit team? Naval Oversight? We kill them now, or they are on your bond, yes?"

Naval Oversight hit team? Menard's head was whirling as he crossed himself. "I… I cannot…."

The very large woman shook her head

imperceptibly.

"Yes," he said, catching the hint. "They are on my... my bond." How in Heaven's name was he going to manage that?

"Good answer, Chor Episcopos." She leaned close. "Is it that you will be celebrating the Mass, Your Reverence? I am wanting of the confessional, myself, and perhaps others here also."

"Ah... of course my... my... child. A priest is always with God." Maybe this was the guidance he had sought in prayer. "Ah... do you know of *Jenny's Little Pearl*? Or Ser Albrecht?"

She shrugged. "I am not hearing of them." Then she handed him back his helmet. "If you are wishing to continue the breathing, to put this on." Pressure alarms were already wailing as he clipped his helmet into place and turned to face his prisoners.

Prisoners?

Naval Oversight. Menard shuddered, a cold weight in his chest.

#

Ten minutes later Menard had been confined within an overtall, narrow storeroom. The guard had deposited him in here, then departed to leave the priest briefly alone with an array of shipping containers stacked at odd angles, secured against the microgravity. He'd spent a few moments contemplating recent events and ignoring the ache in his knees, until the recent combatants arrived with another round of guards and a couple of too-casual medics. They hustled about, focusing mostly on the very small, very dark, very angry woman suffering from a severe crushing blow to the chest, vacuum burn across several puncture wounds, blood loss, and two dislocated hips. She had been stripped to the skin and strapped to a board. Menard tried not to call attention to her shame by his glances, but suspected this woman knew no shame. Her overmuscled, sullen companion cradled his arm and refused assistance. No one wanted to go near the angel, which was sticky-netted to a shipping crate, where it was folded over emitting a strange whine, like a distressed power converter.

The woman stared at Menard as if her eyes had cutting edges, but stayed silent 'til the medics sprayed up her wounds, packed their crash bags, and departed.

"Who the hell are you?" she asked in a pained, wobbly voice as soon as the locals were out of the room.

"I'm the reason you're still alive," he snapped, still rattled. "You may call me Chor Episcopos Menard." He was immediately ashamed of his aggressiveness, but something in her attitude brought out the worst in Menard.

"And that… abomination?" She tried to turn her head to look at the angel, but her neck muscles apparently weren't cooperating. "One of the Patriarch's finest?"

"Not many people survive an argument with an angel."

"Golliwog took care of it," she said with a sharp satisfaction.

The sullen man nodded slowly.

"And you…?" Menard asked. "I've saved your life twice in the past fifteen minutes. Surely I am entitled to know who it is I have gone to this trouble for."

"Captain Yee, Naval Oversight." She took a deep, shuddering breath as pain flickered across her face. "I suspect we may not be working at cross-purposes, Chor Episcopos."

Of course. "Micah Albrecht."

She worked to control another wave of pain. Then: "What do you want him for?"

"Ah," said Menard. "I am free to walk away. You are under my recognizance. Answer me your own question first, then I will tell you." This was sort of like budget meetings back at the Xenic Bureau, except with real blood.

Yet more shudders, passing through her in waves. Golliwog pushed off from his crate, drifted toward Yee's board with an odd light in his eyes. She tried to speak, "I... I... Golliwog...." Her eyes flickered, fighting for consciousness, then she slipped away into some private sea of distress.

"She said anything that happened to her would happen to me first." Golliwog's voice was surprisingly high and thin for such a big man.

Menard looked him over carefully, searching for details. Golliwog had very fleshy features, signs of severe hormone tuning in childhood, but there were also telltale straight lines in muscles of his neck. And he carried himself tightly, with an almost literally artificial stance. Close kin to the angel, in a sense.

The Chor Episcopos knew what he faced—a test, of faith and reason both. "You're a bione, aren't you?" he asked, trying to keep the fear and horror from his voice.

Cybernetically enhanced from human stock, biones were, if anything, a greater abomination than angels. They started out as human, after all, though the Prime See had never formally ruled on what became of their souls under the knives and drugs. Such as this miserable creature went against the nature of both God and man. God's creation, tampered with for man's imperfect purposes.

At the same time, he felt ashamed once more. He had traveled with an angel, after all, no more human than a cat. How could he find horror in this creature made from the flesh of man?

Golliwog nodded. "And you're a priest, aren't you?" he said, in almost the same tone.

"Yes." Then, almost unwilling: "Do you need a priest, my son?"

To Menard's shock, a tear gathered in Golliwog's eye, diamond-bright and no less cutting. "I am no one's son."

A seeker, thought Menard. *This one knows the absence of God in his heart*. He reached out toward Golliwog's tear, knowing he risked life itself in touching this killer. With his index finger, Menard traced a chrism on the monster's forehead. His hand trembled, his back shivered.

Perhaps this was why God had sent him to this place. To minister in this prison to this one man.

For he knew that anyone who cried for salvation must be a man.

The hatch opened and the redheaded woman looked in. "Please to speak to the priest. The freaks to be staying inside, yes? Everyone live longer that way."

Menard broke off his contact, reluctant to abandon a soul in such wretched need, but mindful of the realities of the situation. Caesar had come calling.

Golliwog slipped backward but snagged the cuff of Menard's skinsuit. "Military-grade combat nano out there, priest," he muttered in a low, squeaky tone. "The people here are more dangerous than you know, to be able to have that. Beware."

"Thank you, my son." Menard nodded as he drifted toward the hatch. "And may the Lord bless you and keep you."

He found himself praying for… for… well, everything. And everyone.

#

Golliwog: Halfsummer Solar Space, The Necklace, Shorty's Surprise

Golliwog watched the priest leave. The little man had one last frightened, backward glance from the hatch before the musclegirl outside took him away. A priest, a real priest. Someone who had tried to tell him whether he had a soul, to help him understand whether God cared about him. His forehead tingled with the drying salt of that single tear.

What had that meant? For one single moment, there had been light in his head.

Freedom, whispered the traitor voice within. *Freedom to choose, to be.*

There was so much he didn't know, yet.

Golliwog shook off the thought and took a long look at Yee. Instead of small and tough, she just seemed to be small and dying. He was amazed she'd fought the pain and the drugs the medics had given her long enough to speak to the priest at all. Now she had left him alone.

It was the first time in his life he'd been alone. Truly alone, out of command, with no controller.

He wondered whether the priest had truly cared for him, however briefly. Weren't they supposed to act that way toward everyone? The Navy had chaplains, shiploads of them he supposed, but no chaplain had ever been the least bit interested in the state of Golliwog's conscience. Assuming he had one. At least he knew what the word meant—inner moral judgment.

Golliwog turned his back on Yee and kicked himself toward the angel. His right forearm was still dead in both of its aspects, meat and metal. That thing was too dangerous to be allowed to live. Nothing should have been able to trump him so thoroughly. He braced his good hand on the crate above the angel's sticky-netting. Trapped in the fat, oozing strands, it continued to keen, bent over as if something had been snapped within.

He damned well hoped something had been snapped within. Now he needed to finish the job.

Something pulsed on the carrier frequency in his head. Was it trying to talk? Then the angel forced its head to move against the webbing, rotating that narrow white face slightly toward Golliwog. The red cross on its scalp seemed to throb. Red eyes blinked open, smearing tears of blood.

Tears. This thing cried. Pain, sorrow, regret. He had no idea what or why, but this angel cried.

In that moment, Golliwog could not kill it. Not tied down and crying. Not after what the priest had just shown him about himself. To be human was to choose not to kill.

Kill it he would, if need be—facing the angel once more in open combat, for example. He would kill God himself if the Creator came after Golliwog with a knife in His hand and murder in His eye. But not now, he could not slay the angel while it existed as a wounded experiment strapped to a crate. He knew the horror of being a made thing. After all, he was terrified of Yee cutting him open to work out whatever it was that had happened during c-transit.

"Soon," he told the angel, though Golliwog was fairly certain he was lying even to himself. "Soon we will be free, and we will make good our pain upon the man who led us here."

The angel's mouth opened, blood bubbles popping out, then it sighed and closed its face.

#

Albrecht: Halfsummer Solar Space, The Necklace, Shorty's Surprise

He stared in amazement, one of Dillon's paws upon his arm, as the bar's patrons stripped the wood away from three of the triangles comprising the dodecahedron. It was obviously designed to come apart. Underneath was a huge painting—a mural?—of a starship. The image was intended to represent something here in the Halfsummer system, given the bright silver braid that was The Necklace crossing the sky behind the ship.

He found the details hard to assess. The painter had been no artist, but was obviously driven to render this image by some powerful inner fire. A better hand with the paint might have helped, though.

"This was in the original Shorty's Bar," rumbled Dillon. "Been there seventy, eighty years. When we finally scrapped that module, we salvaged the art and brought the panels in here. Built this version of the bar around them."

Albrecht was fascinated by the sheer obsessiveness of the thing. The painting was about ten meters wide, rendered in a level of detail that spoke of years of effort. He wondered, if he looked closely enough, would he be able to count the explosive bolts on the hull segment joints? And the vessel in question was huge, inasmuch as scale could be judged in something as impressionistic as a painting. There were recognizable structures—radiator towers, for example—that implied that the ship was impossibly large.

It was all... wrong... though. Cocked into unrecognizability by a hundred mistaken visual and engineering cues. Like someone who'd been told about right angles but never personally experienced one had decided to illustrate a text on plane geometry.

"What ship is it supposed to be?" he finally asked. "Is it real?"

A sharp breath from Dillon. Then: "We thought you could tell us. It's called the Poolyard, hereabouts."

"*Poolyard*'s the name of the ship?" Albrecht asked.

"No. The painter." Dillon rumbled through a snort which might have been a laugh at one time in its history. "Stumbled in to the old Shorty's blind as a pulsed-out sensor array. Talked about colors a lot, for a blind guy. Screamed, too."

"In his sleep?"

"No, just in general."

"Right." Albrecht glanced at his companion. "May I look closer?"

Dillon tightened his grip on Albrecht's arm and kicked them both off to drift across the central core of the bar.

He studied the picture with a careful eye to the details of size. "If those cooling towers are to any kind of scale, that thing's several kilometers long. Nothing was ever built that big except stage-one colonial transports and those dictator-class pre-Imperial battle—" He suddenly stopped talking as Dillon's grip tightened to a crush. "Oh…."

"Yes," said Dillon.

Albrecht winced. "So why do people want to kill me?"

"Because you know where it is."

"Like hell!" Then he thought about that a moment. "*Jenny D*. The… virus. What people live and die for." And the ephemeris on *Pearl*.

God damn it. He'd left the key to an entire pre-Imperial battlewagon parked out there, defended only by an angry newt.

"Yes," said Dillon. He nodded. The rest of the bar began reassembling the floor panels. The big man then grabbed a brass stanchion and slingshotted the two of them back toward their original table.

"It's not really that big a secret, out here in The Necklace. That she exists, I mean. No one admits to knowing where. She's cold-parked in some eccentric orbit, that's obvious. It's implied clearly enough in the painting, if you look at the angle of view on The Necklace. High up, out of the plane of the ecliptic. And if she was anywhere simple, that battlewagon would have been found long ago. There's always some idiot thinks that bringing her back into the light might be a good idea."

Albrecht nodded. "I wouldn't count on the painting for much in the way of useful perspective. It's crude as a child's work."

"Oh, Poolyard painted what he saw."

"I thought you said he was blind."

"Well, yes, there's a problem, isn't it?"

Albrecht glared at Dillon. "Does this riddle have a valve-bleeding answer? Or are you just going to stay all cryptic on me until the bad guys shoot their way in?"

"The bad guys have already gotten here," Dillon said. "They're otherwise engaged at this moment."

"But both ships are hours out!"

"They each sent pathfinders. It's been ugly outside." Dillon grabbed Albrecht's arm again. "Not your concern, not yet."

"Fine," said Albrecht. "That's the past. It's cold, it's dead, no one knows where it is except me, and whoever recorded the data I've gotten hold of. And whoever copied it out for backup. And whoever has maintained *Pearl*'s systems in the past decade. But that's a secret. I get it." He pried Dillon's fingers off him, glaring again. "So you asked me about the future. What does a dead battleship mean to your future? You planning to crank up another Civil War?"

"Not if its humanly possible to avoid it," said Dillon sadly, with some trace of irony. "Don't want one, don't need one. Wouldn't matter anyway. That thing gets found, put back together, she outslugs any twenty percent of the Imperial Navy all massed together. Won't be a Civil War. No one could stop her fully armed and under way. Question is, what would follow? Making a new order would be damn near impossible, but anyone could smash the existing peace with that ship. They built them big, in the old days."

"I know, I know." Albrecht could see where sitting on something like this would give a man a case of the gray gumps. "Ship types are sort of a hobby of mine. The dictators were decommissioned for a lot of reasons, cost not the least of them, but sheer disarmament was a big one too. There's no one to fight but each other, why make it too easy? I get it. But what does this have to do with *me?*"

Dillon's face darkened. "There's some who want to bring her into a yard. Do some work on her. 'Insurance,' they call it."

"Who's got a shipyard big enough for that monster?"

"Us. God help us, we built one that big, just in case."

Albrecht slapped the table, propelling himself upward. Why had he thought for a moment that these folk might have a better future in mind, with their sweaty kids and crowded station? They were as violent and venal as anyone else, parking death and destruction out in the Deep Dark to await another day. "You people are idiots."

Dillon tugged Albrecht back down. "We're *human*, Ser Albrecht. We disagree with one another. We make choices. We make mistakes. We learn."

"And now you want to learn how to get rid of it." The light bloomed in Albrecht's thoughts. "You want me to find it, do something, so you don't have to go through a Naval Oversight investigation into why you've been hiding a battleship all these decades." His voice pitched up. "So I can patsy it into the open, turn the thing over to Lieutenant Bourne or those Church goons who are chasing me. Then somebody bigger and badder shows up, sweeps the mess under the rug, and goes away. That works for you, doesn't it? Otherwise that damned ship gets found some other way, sooner or later. Then everybody's staring at the belters of The Necklace, asking what the hell your plans were anyway!"

"Yes," said Dillon simply. "I'm sorry, but that's all true. We need you to help us lose it into plain sight. You followed me down here, through the core of Shorty's Surprise. You've seen our people. Our *children*. We've created too much here in the last century to trip over an old idea about mounting some pointless rebellion."

That was certainly true. *"Then who built the damned shipyard!?"*

"People with other ideas, Ser Albrecht. People with other ideas."

"You know," Albrecht began quietly. He stopped, sipped from his sugar water. "All I ever wanted was get out of here."

"You're far too late to avoid taking some kind of fall. Everyone in the system knows your name, the Navy and the Church are both after you, and the Imperial Resident's in line behind them waiting for his turn. We're just asking that you steer that fall to land somewhere that doesn't point right back toward us. And take that battleship with you on the way."

"Yeah, well." He was back to having no future at all. He *had* been a dead man sailing, these last few days. "I guess that means I need to find my way out there."

"Soon, Ser Albrecht. You must leave before the superior firepower arrives."

"Am I on my own?"

"No." Dillon smiled. "We'll take my rock hopper. And I think we'll have a third set of hands along."

Some of his anger bled away at the thought of Dillon coming along. Albrecht didn't know the monstrous man, not in any way that made sense, but if Dillon were coming, he meant what he was saying.

Trust had been a rare commodity in Albrecht's life of late, ever since his abrupt departure from *Princess Janivera*. But there was something in Dillon that he wanted to trust. "Fine. I need some data off *Jenny's Little Pearl*. I locked the systems from the console. We have to go back on board so I can override." *And Christ*, he thought, *that damned newt was still out there*.

"Are you willing to pass the boat's codes to me? I have people who might be able to hack that out while we're preparing. If not, well, we start our journey there."

Albrecht sighed. He popped the codelock key out of his thigh pack. "Here you go. It's bearer-driven, no biometrics or encoding. They didn't want complications, when they set this up. *Idiots*."

"Humans."

"Whatever. I'd like that back, in working order please."

"Certainly." Dillon grabbed one edge of the table, preparing to shove off. "I'll be back shortly. This is as safe as anywhere on Shorty's Surprise for you right now. Stay here. Anyone comes to see you, they've been cleared."

"Whatever."

Dillon launched himself across a chord of the arc of the dodecahedron, heading for the hatch to the chaos outside. Albrecht nursed his sugar water and tried to figure out whether he had any path through this that didn't end badly.

Hell, he'd been living on borrowed time since *Novy Petrograd* showed up. He was *days* ahead at this point. And maybe there was still hope after all.

#

Some time later, after Albrecht had given in to something distilled and far too high proof for his own good, a near-twin of Dillon, but with drifting red hair—a clone clutch, like he'd first thought?—popped through the bar's hatch towing a stubby, stocky priest dressed in a helmetless skinsuit. The newcomer looked something between angry and frightened. The Dillon-clone pointed Albrecht out to the priest, gave the short man a good hard toss, and dropped back through the hatch.

To Albrecht's surprise, the priest managed his way through the arc without spinning out of control, and hooked into the table unassisted.

"Father," Albrecht said neutrally.

"It's Chor Episcopos, actually," the priest snapped. "The Reverend Chor Episcopos Jonah Menard."

Of course. "You've been looking for me, I believe."

Menard's face opened. "Ah. Please forgive my surliness. The past hours have not been easy, even for a forgiving heart. You are Micah Albrecht? Of *Jenny's Diamond Bright*?"

"Not exactly, but close. The same man you laid a Writ of Attainder on. Your Reverence."

"It kept you alive," Menard pointed out. "I wasn't ready to lose you to *Novy Petrograd*."

"Who am I to you? Why'd they dump you on me? Or vice versa."

"Why'd they put us together? Maybe because I didn't try to kill anyone on arrival." The priest gripped the table, his knuckles pale. "As to who you are… you're the man who knows about *Jenny D*. Are you going out to the ship? They said I was to go with you."

Albrecht had to laugh. He had no idea the Church had an angle on insurance fraud. Or conspiracy to rebellion, whichever this really was. "Oh no, it's much worse than that, Chor Episcopos. I thought I knew where *Jenny D* was, but we seem to have hooked a far bigger fish here."

"I'm hunting the biggest fish of all, Ser Albrecht."

"I doubt it. I've seen this fish, and with all respect, Your Reverence, I don't think it's what you are looking for."

"What have you seen, my son?"

"Ah…" Albrecht closed his eyes a moment. This place, he'd seen this place. The distances a man could pass in moments, after standing still for most of a lifetime. "The past. The future. I'm not sure, truthfully. If you're coming with me, you'll find out soon enough. If you're not coming with me, it doesn't matter anyway."

Menard frowned. He'd obviously played this game before. "I seem to be missing my angel. I cannot abandon a servant of the Patriarch."

"Your… angel?"

"My, ah, enforcer. Sword and hand of the Lord. It has been injured."

"I don't know about any angels, Chor Episcopos, but this will probably be worth the ride." Albrecht took a deep breath, then: "I hope to God it is." For the sake of a lot of people.

"Strangely, so do I."

#

Menard: Halfsummer Solar Space, The Necklace, Shorty's Surprise

Micah Albrecht wasn't what he'd expected. For one, the man seemed almost depressingly normal. Menard had spent his career among the highly driven, and occasionally the highly desperate. He'd assumed Albrecht was one or both of those, simply based on the situation here in Halfsummer.

No, Ser Albrecht could have been an average parishioner in an average community anywhere in the Empire. Of middling height, ordinary looks, nothing exceptional about him at all.

Except for the facts of the situation, of course, and that Albrecht had hooked a big fish of some kind.

Menard wondered whether he was close to a breakthrough on the xenic question. To what degree were they really among the human race? Was Albrecht involved with xenics? Sister Pelias's K-M curves had led Menard here to Halfsummer, further into the question than he'd ever been able to go before.

But as always, he wondered who was playing whom.

Albrecht had gone silent, sullen, unwilling to divulge more about whatever his end of the secret was. Having come this far, Menard was willing to be patient.

He worried about the angel, though, with a rippling sense of guilt. Bishop Russe had charged him with the creature, and the angel with him. Would Captain Yee and her creature have killed Menard out of hand if the angel hadn't been there? It had moved first, but for a reason... what?

Ser Albrecht certainly wouldn't know that. Who would? Angels didn't, well... talk.

He needed to know why the angel had attacked. And whether it could continue onward with him. Unfortunately for Menard, he was the leading authority on angels in localspace. No one else could help him.

Oh, Lord, prayed Menard silently, *Your humble servant begs Your guidance in this hour of my need. I am troubled by the fate of Your angel, and my duty tells me to stay by it and seek to heal it. At the same time my heart tells me I must follow the path of this Micah Albrecht, as he may lead me toward my life's work. I do not know whether You have set the xenics in the path of man as a stepping-stone or a stumbling block, but I know You will reveal Your will to me when the time is right. But in this moment, oh my Creator, Your will is not clear. What path shall I choose? Please, Lord, I beg of You a sign.*

Glory to the Father, and to the Son, and to the Holy Spirit, now and ever and unto ages of ages. Amen.

He looked up to see Albrecht staring at him. "I'm a priest, my son," Menard said gently. "I pray. It's what we do."

"Does God answer?"

"Generally, yes, if I have but the wisdom to hear it."

A near-twin of the redheaded woman, but male and bald, took that moment to pop through the hatch and propel himself across the bar straight toward them, two helmets dangling from one hand. "Now would be an excellent time to leave, gentlemen," he said in a gear-crushing voice as he tossed them both their headgear.

"Nice to see you, too, Dillon," said Albrecht. "Have you met Chor Episcopos Menard?"

Dillon nodded briefly, agitated. The man was sweating, even, which was odd in the perpetually chill environment of a station. "I know who he is. Ser Albrecht, there's been an internal disagreement here on Shorty's Surprise. I have lost the codelock key. Irretrievable. We should exit quickly, before we become irretrievably lost as well."

And here, thought Menard with a surge of guilty relief with respect to the fate of the angel, *is God's sign. Thank you, Lord. Forgive me my ill feelings toward*

Your fellow servant. But the Captain and her bione were under his protection. "I cannot go—" he began, when he was interrupted.

"Did you get the damned ephemeris?" Albrecht snapped, his face flushing with anger. Or was it fear?

Dillon looked back and forth at the two of them. "No time to argue. We've got the data, the key is gone from us." The big man coiled to spring back toward the hatch. "*Now*, Albrecht."

"Coming, Chor Episcopos?" Albrecht asked.

"I do not have a choice." Crossing himself, Menard launched after the other two men in an eddy of their fear-scent and anger. He needed to follow this lead to xenics even more than he needed to maintain his "prisoners." From whom he had been separated.

Surely the belters of Shorty's Surprise would take care of them.

He promised himself they would. On his word.

Please, God.

#

Golliwog: Halfsummer Solar Space, The Necklace, Shorty's Surprise

Thirty-two minutes and seventeen point four four zero one seconds after the priest had departed, the hatch cycled open. Golliwog held himself in check in a far corner of the store room. His legs were folded, ready to spring, and he had his dead left arm bound to his aching side, out of harm's way. He would not attack without reason or orders, even if he had to give himself the reasons and the orders.

That was a novel thought. He stored it with the other tokens of his rebellion as someone tossed a heavy package through the hatch then cycled it shut again.

Bomb!

Golliwog hurled himself across the space. If there

was a timer, he might be able to stop it. If not, he could shield Yee and the angel from the blast.

He splayed himself to land over the target, forgetting his lashed arm. Off point, Golliwog wound up taking weight on his left shoulder and smacking into the package. It was hard, unyielding, painful against his already distressed ribs and gut. It was not, however, explosive.

Yet.

He curled around it, his back to Yee and the package in the curve of his body. Steadying it with one foot, he touched it lightly with his right hand. Vacuum-rated utility cloth, folded and secured with a molecular clamp. No code on the clamp, just a release button.

Another arming option, of course. Press the release button, go boom. But he wouldn't get at any interior wiring any other way. He clenched his bowels and pressed.

The cloth package popped open. Tools, three smaller bags with carry straps. No bomb. Or if it was a bomb, it was a rather baroque approach to bomb-making.

Inventory, Golliwog told himself.

One: Bladed hand tool he didn't recognize, with a chemical dispenser built in and a reservoir clipped to the butt end. Cutter for the angel's web restraints, perhaps? Certainly a decent weapon in a fight.

Two: Field-grade surgical spidersilk applicator. Used for wound closure. Someone expected him to get hurt.

Three: A battered civilian-grade codelock key, for access to equipment with manual lockdowns. In this context, either a station segment or a boat outside in the deep ark. Golliwog had a good idea which boat that might be. And that was a positive development, because it wasn't possible to fit both Yee and the angel into the little black boat he and Yee had arrived in.

Four: A small fléchette pistol. Almost no butt. Less accurate but much easier to carry unnoticed. He spared it a closer glance. Bioplastics. Depending on the materials used to make the pressurized valvework and control circuits, this might even walk through a passive security scan without setting off alarms. Dangerous, in more ways than the obvious.

Two of the smaller bags turned out to be life bubbles—inflatable pods designed to allow low-competence or unrated users to survive in vacuum. These were extremely low-end, toys really, with twenty-minute safety ratings and ten-minute margins beyond that.

Not at all to his surprise, the last bag contained a disposable skinsuit with a baggie-style helmet. About the same utility value as the life bubbles, except for the zero value of breathing vacuum as an alternative.

Someone wanted him to leave, and to tow his two wounded with him. Golliwog would have bet his good arm that the codelock key gave him access to *Jenny's Little Pearl*. His unknown benefactors wanted him off Shorty's Surprise.

Another bet Golliwog would make was that his time window was critically short.

He wondered briefly about the priest. They had taken Chor Episcopos Menard away, just when Golliwog thought he might have found... what? Interest? Attention? Focus from a human being who was motivated neither by fear nor by their role in the command chain? It didn't matter. He owed Menard nothing.

The angel was another matter. Made things had nothing, were nothing. He didn't know whether he was saving or condemning it, but he would set it free. If it died, it died on its own terms, not glued to a crate somewhere.

Golliwog worked his way over to the angel. His guess was right; the cutting tool worked on the restraint webbing. The blade cut into the semisolid dynamic polymer, while the chemical slime behind it dissolved the bonds that otherwise reset instantly. He cut the angel free, not trying to deal with the web strands clinging to its red armor and dead-white skin. Those weird, gossamer wings that had hurt him so badly were gone, folded back to whatever virtual space inside the angel's body—or head—from which they had come. He dragged it into one of the life bubbles. He waited to pop the seals. After all, it would be beyond stupid to use up the reserves while still inside the station.

Dr. Yee was next. Golliwog launched the bagged-up angel on a slow arc toward the hatch, then made his way to the board where she was still strapped. He wondered how she would feel if he began cutting into her, to see how she worked, what she was made of.

But the station medics had been cutting into her, spraying little repairs into place to hold her guts together, reinflating her lungs, setting her hips back where she belonged. What would he achieve?

"If I take you now," he told the unconscious Yee, "we are even. You do not own me any more. Setting you free, I set myself free."

Her eyes flickered at his voice. "Kill it now," she whispered, though she still didn't seem to be conscious.

"Not yet," he said. "But soon. That's a promise."

Golliwog used the webbing cutter to slice through Yee's straps, then slid her into the other life bubble. He sliced some tie-downs loose from nearby crates and lashed the two life bubbles together. After that, he stripped off his old skinsuit—they had taken the helmet away when they'd imprisoned him here—and pulled on the disposable unit. Stuffing the tools into one of the utility bags, he towed his charges to the hatch and slapped the button.

It slid open. He found himself completely unsurprised.

#

Albrecht: Halfsummer Solar Space, The Necklace, Shorty's Surprise

They moved fast through the station, amid the smells and sounds and movements of thousands of crowded human beings. Albrecht followed Dillon, who had picked up the largest ballspitter he'd ever seen. The priest struggled along behind, but kept up. People who saw them coming through the tall, crowded caves of humanity got out of the way. There were a few struggles as some kept others from interfering.

"Coup?" Albrecht panted with the effort of their rapid flight.

"Disagreement," Dillon said shortly. "Past versus future."

"Black Flag."

A grunt from ahead of Albrecht.

Then they were in a utility passageway. Dillon snap-spun to orient himself feet forward on their direction of travel and loosed a burst from the ballspitter. The high-elasticity projectiles rattled and thumped as they shot down the passageway, to a startled yelp from ahead, as Dillon staggered in his flight before recovering his forward momentum.

Albrecht was starting to feel a "down" to the right. He grabbed a rung, twisted himself ninety degrees, and adopted the long, low-gravity lope of a spaceman. They came to a hatch in what was now the floor without further opposition.

Dillon turned. "Listen. It's point three gees at the bottom of this shaft, about a hundred meters down. You lose control, it's going to hurt on impact. Kill you if you come down wrong. *Don't screw up*."

He didn't wait for an answer, just keyed the hatch open to an underlit hole with a faint red glow, like distant fire down below. Dillon dropped in with one hand on a ladder rail and the other aiming his ballspitter downward.

Albrecht waved Menard in next. "I'll follow, Chor Episcopos."

"Bless you, my son. Fall safely." Menard, for all that his face showed his nerves, kicked himself over the hatch lip headfirst like a Marine, reaching for the rail as he went.

Albrecht glanced up the corridor to see someone with a fléchette rifle watching him. At least they weren't shooting. Right now, anything was possible. Worlds turned on moments like this. He waved maniacally, then followed the priest headfirst, swallowing his stomach.

The hatch cycled shut behind them.

#

He hit bottom hard enough to wish he hadn't. Chor Episcopos Menard had gotten out of the way, thankfully, and was hustling spinward through the girdered shadows of some ancient equipment bay toward another open hatch, red-lit in the floor.

"I believe this is Ser Dillon's rock hopper," Menard said with a glance over his shoulder.

Albrecht looked around. This space had been something different once, though he had no idea what. Now it was filled with groaning masses of metal and carbonmesh chained against the coreward bulkheads, straining with the force of the rotation. A third of a gee was enough to send something loose sailing outward at close to three meters per second per second. He didn't want to think about how many tons were hanging over his head, great blunt Damoclean plowshares. If there was a problem, they couldn't just turn off the gravimetrics and shift things looking for his body.

Something clanged in the distance, as Dillon bellowed unintelligibly from below.

"Go," said Albrecht.

Menard went. Albrecht followed.

#

Gravity was wrong inside. They were being pulled toward what should have been the bow. The crash couches were set perpendicular to the current normal plane. Dillon was already strapped into the central seat, his ballspitter racked above his head. Albrecht noted that the barrel was pointing straight at him and the hatch behind.

"Strap in, now," said Dillon. "We're twenty-four seconds from drop."

Menard was clambering awkwardly down into the portside seat, so Albrecht dropped onto the starboard seat. "Where's the rest of the boat?" This cabin was smaller than *Pearl*'s bridge, about forty percent of the bulkheads actually translucent panels that currently showed a crisscross of cables and girders. They were going to launch into *that?*

"This is it. Secure for drop."

"Secured," said Menard.

Albrecht finished clicking his mechanical restraints in place. "Starboard seat secured." Looking around, he saw his hardsuit lashed in just forward of the hatch he'd tumbled through. Someone had thought ahead. He wondered where the cash had gotten to, then felt vaguely ashamed of the thought.

"Seven... six..." Someone began banging on the hatch as a hull section slid open in front of them, showing the glittering fog of Shorty's Surprise localspace beyond. "Fuck... you... three... two... one..." Dillon pulled a red toggle with a strain that had to be spring-locked. There was a very loud clang, then the apparent gravity essentially reversed, going from tugging Albrecht forward against his straps to pulling him backward and slightly up as they tumbled screaming into the bright fog of active defense nano.

#

Golliwog: Halfsummer Solar Space, The Necklace, Shorty's Surprise

It was a strange exit. He had made it from the storeroom into the passageways unchallenged. The life bubbles massed, of course, but they didn't pull in any particular direction in the microgravity at Shorty's core. He'd worked his way toward the skin, fighting the increasing pull of Yee and the angel—who were both thankfully light on mass—until he'd run into another pair of those giant men. The fléchette pistol had gutted them before they realized who he was, but alarms hooted moments after.

He had to assume the bells tolled for him.

Someone was herding Golliwog, though. Some hatches opened at his approach, others stayed resolutely shut even when he banged on emergency overrides. He'd found himself in an elevator shaft, a skeletal little car wrapped around a ten-centimeter cable that glittered of woven diamond carbonmesh. One of the rockball cables, of course.

He'd taken the hint, sealed all three life support systems and begun counting minutes. The cage left a little clanking airlock, the noise of which faded with the air pressure, lifting him against gravity into the whirling junk cloud around Shorty's Surprise. From inside the elevator, the rockballs and the huge, cluttered central cylinder appeared absolutely steady, while The Necklace beyond them moved quickly enough to catch his eye. Scanning the area, Golliwog watched another hatch further around the sidewall arc of the central core open.

A stubby, fat-tailed boat shot out of Shorty's Surprise. It spun twice, trailing bright fire in the glittering fog, then thrusters puffed as the boat oriented itself and made a course clear of the whirling rockballs, the multiple parked ships, and the general chaos of localspace here.

"Good-bye, Ser Albrecht," he whispered into the collapsed bag of his disposable helmet. "We will meet soon." With that, the elevator fell into a hole in the rockball beneath his feet.

Time to find a way out. *Jenny's Little Pearl* awaited.

#

The rockball was crazy-crowded, interior laid out in marked contrast to the purposeful architecture of the core. It was another country, so to speak, where people moved in groups and gangs, and air seemed to be sold by the minute or the day. There was gravity here, too much of it frankly, but the corridors twisted and coiled in defiance. They were lined with ropes and cables and ladders and cargo nets, a sort of infinite gymnasium inhabited by the hungry and the hopeless.

As oddly patched and put together as the core had been, Shorty's balls were dark and dangerous, and filled with dark, dangerous people. No wonder they'd grown them big back in the core.

Golliwog struggled through the heavier gravity with the life bubbles slung over his left shoulder, connecting cable wrapped once around his left arm. He let the pistol show in his right hand. Everything else was stuffed in the utility bag over his right shoulder.

He was conscious of the minutes remaining. Minutes 'til the life ran out of canned air and heat. Minutes 'til his disposable suit gave up. Minutes that Albrecht was almost certainly using to get away. Golliwog didn't care about the mythical *Enver Hoxha*. He didn't care about *Jenny D*. He just wanted out.

Stay here, whispered the rebel voice in his head.

Golliwog shrugged it off and worked his way toward the lighter gravity of the coreward hemisphere. Stepping out of a hatch on the spinward side would simply cause him to repeat Albrecht's departure from the core, except without the benefit of a spaceship wrapped around his body. Stepping out on the coreward side would allow him to control his jumping-off point.

He held something between a hope and a prayer that he could recognize and make his way to *Jenny's Little Pearl* in the few minutes that remained to him and his charges by the time he got back into vacuum. It struck Golliwog that his unknown benefactors had already accomplished their aims. He was out of the core, as were Yee and the angel, and Albrecht was gone, too. There was no guarantee they'd given him enough air, tools, and supplies to make his own climb.

Stop now, said that voice, *and live among these hard men a while. You'll find a place, they'll welcome your talents once they stop trying to kill you. Yee and the angel are done, and who is Albrecht to you? What are those missing ships to you?*

The priest. The priest who had called him "son" would expect more. Golliwog owed the priest nothing, either, but… he had to start somewhere. He knew he wasn't going back, but he could do his job before he left. He would be more than a piece of equipment, more than a weapon, whatever law and regs said about biones.

Whether the Navy would recognize his departure was another issue entirely, but he would blow that airlock when he came to it.

And here was one final upward climb, a shoal of starving-thin boys scattering at a spray of needles from Golliwog's pistol. He tucked the weapon into the lashed fold of his left arm and began the last one-handed ascent. Even here, in two-thirds gravity, it was a strain. Had he been an ordinary human, Golliwog would already have failed.

#

The top of the ladder was indeed an airlock, some strange helical design ripped from a long-vanished ship and welded into place here. Like all the other hatches inside the rockball, it opened at the press of a button. Whatever security they had here certainly wasn't enforced by architecture or facilities design.

This lock had a long, tubular chamber. Had it once fired projectiles, he wondered? Ignoring the burning in his chest, Golliwog hauled the life bubbles to the top as the air pumped out, then opened the last hatch.

The view above was wrenching. Shorty's core was absolutely still two hundred meters above his head, filling the central arc of his personal sky. The other two balls were visible beyond it. Various ships and hulks kept some kind of position with respect to the primary. The rest of the world rotated, the bright ribbon of The Necklace moving visibly.

Fourteen minutes, eleven point four seconds since he'd activated the angel's life bubble. Yee was seven seconds behind. Well within the margin of error of the crude systems.

When they'd parked the dark boat, Golliwog and Yee had spotted *Jenny's Little Pearl* tucked against some old mass hauler. *That* hulk wasn't hard to find now, either. It was the biggest thing in localspace after Shorty's balls and the core of the Surprise itself. It was between his current and the next rockball, more or less.

He tried to calculate the jumping-off vector and velocity he'd require to make the leap, realized he simply didn't know his own mass with enough precision. Not when the mass included Yee and the angel hanging from his body. And this damned suit had no thrusters at all. Another flaw to go with its five minutes of air.

The first time Golliwog had ever tried to play catch, as a juvenile, he'd nearly had a seizure calculating intercepts and probability curves. Humans, true humans, didn't calculate trajectories. They just leapt and trusted.

He was good now, too. Better than any human, even one as overtrained as Dr. Yee. But this was a time to leap and trust: himself, Chor Episcopos Menard's God, whatever fate there was that watched over him.

"And so I jump," said Golliwog. He closed his eyes and kicked off, the most human act he had ever committed.

#

Golliwog opened his eyes again. He was at least making headway toward the mass hauler. He was also falling away, in a natural reaction to the angular momentum imparted him by Shorty's ball. Nano glittered around him as the defensive cloud reacted to his passage. It had trapped Golliwog once before, immobilizing him to be hauled into the core after his fight with the angel.

He tried his carrier signal again. He wanted to modulate the nano formations, get them to accumulate on his rimward side, millions of tiny thrusters each exercising a few millimeter/milligrams of thrust to correct his arc toward the mass hauler.

Once more the fog rippled at his mental touch, but he didn't see the Naval countersigns. It was hacked, or homebrewed, he already knew that, but the fact that it reacted to him meant the underlying tech was similar.

It didn't matter. His course was moving further and

further away from the target. In about thirty-five seconds he would pass a point of no return, where there wasn't any reasonable correction to bring him back to the mass hauler and to *Jenny's Little Pearl*.

What was left to him?

What was left to any human *in extremis?*

"God," Golliwog said, his voice muffled inside his baggie helmet. "You are not for me, and I am not Your creation. But if your priest Menard saw something of worth in me, perhaps You do too."

Nothing happened. He became angry at the thought of dying, of wasting himself out here.

"Move, damn it!" he shouted at the nano. He could see the point of no return on his trajectory fast approaching. "Move!"

Inspiration struck. Golliwog grabbed the pistol from where it was tucked inside his dead left arm. He aimed it opposite his desired line of travel, into the axis of thrust he wanted from the nano. It might react, it might trap him, shred him, shock him, do nothing.

"Hey God! Are you listening?" Twenty-four seconds from the point of no return, Golliwog pulled the trigger.

#

Menard: Halfsummer Solar Space, The Necklace, In transit

It was a while before the inside of Dillon's rock hopper stopped smelling like rank, dank fear. Menard had been inside prisons more pleasant than this. To his right, Albrecht rubbed his left wrist obsessively and muttered. All he could see of Dillon was a three-quarter rear profile of the pilot's crash couch, and most of Dillon's left arm.

At least gravity was in the floor now, though something hummed with an ozone crackle that fought the fear-stink and promised extended future microgravity.

And the view was amazing. Menard gave thanks to God that the Creator had not seen fit to endow His priest with agoraphobia. Instead, he saw all the diamonds of The Necklace as if they had been arrayed for his delight.

"We just want to get rid of it, you know," Dillon said into the long silence that had stretched since launch. "Well, most of us," he added after another thoughtful pause.

"I just wanted out of here," Albrecht answered. "Now I'm the target of multiple manhunts. But…" He stopped, thinking of the people crowded within Shorty's Surprise. "You belters. There's a world and more here, isn't there?"

"The lack of one, more like it," Dillon muttered, but Menard could hear the humor in his voice, matching the tension in Albrecht's tone.

"I never thought to found anything worthwhile in this damned system," Albrecht said quietly. "Speaking of Halfsummer, where's *Novy Petrograd*, anyway?"

"Still hanging around Shorty's, watching *Jenny's Little Pearl*."

"I don't suppose your geniuses wiped that ephemeridian data when they pulled it out."

"No." Dillon's tone suggested further questioning was unwise—that was obvious to Menard. He cut Albrecht off even as the spacer opened his mouth for more. "What are you two talking about?"

"Give me thirty minutes, Chor Episcopos, and I'll show you."

"We're not nearly that close," muttered Albrecht.

"You want to drive?"

"No."

"Then shut up."

"Gentlemen," Menard said slowly in his best staff meeting voice. "We have our lives, and freedom of movement. Whatever, ah, coup, was under way back there did not stop us from making our exit in good order."

"The Black Flag," said Dillon. "Our dark side. This may be putting them over the top."

The top of what, Menard wondered, but he held his counsel. *St. Gaatha* would be on the scene soon enough, and Lieutenant McNally would take a keen interest in learning his whereabouts. Unless whoever was behind Captain Yee from Naval Oversight showed up with a bigger ship, of course. He wondered what had become of her and that wretched bione in the company of the angel. "Do you know the fate of my prisoners?"

"Wrong people got 'em," Dillon snapped. "Could be free, could be dead."

"Ah." Menard bowed his head and began to pray for the souls of the probably departed.

#

A while later Dillon rolled the rock hopper. The sky precessed in front of the view ports until they were facing at a low, reverse angle to their line of travel. "Watch," said Dillon, and tapped a code sequence into one of his panels.

Out there in the Deep Dark, a sequence of blue lights lit up, one after another, a ripple effect that went on for about ten seconds.

It seemed big, and it was blesséd invisible without the lights. There was no way to achieve a sense of scale out here, though.

"What is it?" asked Menard.

"Refitting yard," Albrecht said sourly.

"A yard? For tugs, or ice crackers or some such?"

Albrecht again: "Yes. *Idiots*. Now show him the rest of it, Dillon."

Dillon tapped another sequence. This time, the

lights rippled almost forty seconds. The perspective was much deeper.

"That, Your Reverence," said Albrecht, "is about four kilometers of refitting frames."

"Four kilometers?" Menard was shocked. "And no one ever noticed it?"

"Even the inspectors only come here in our ships," Dillon said. "They use our instruments. No one ever looks out the window in space. Nothing to see."

That made a certain kind of sense. "Unless you're a rock jockey."

"Right."

Four kilometers! Menard tried to work those dimensions out in terms he was familiar with. The Patriarch's personal transport, *Sts. Kyril and Methodius*, had a keel about nine hundred meters long. He'd been told it was the largest starship in the Empire, even bigger than the Emperor's flagship. "So why is it that large? This is your big fish, right, Ser Albrecht?"

"Biggest fish of all. Dictator-class battleship."

"NSS *Enver Hoxha*," said Dillon.

Hoxha. Hoxha. Why did he know that name? "What's a battleship doing here in Halfsummer? What's a battleship doing *anywhere*? They were all scrapped decades ago, before I was born."

"No one knows," said Dillon. "Been here since the Civil War is all I can tell you."

"Bloody idiots need a place to refit her," Albrecht added.

The light of revelation bloomed in Menard's head. It was almost as powerful as that moment when God had driven him to his knees at thirteen, and from there into the priesthood. This was what had shivered his bones back when he had been talking to Russe, when this whole mystery had first begun to unfold. He wanted to sing.

At Your command all things came to be, he thought, *the vast expanse of interstellar space*. Then, in a whisper: "I know."

"I know," he said.

"I know!" he shouted.

Dillon twisted in his chair to look at Menard, as Albrecht gave him a long, sideways stare. "You know what?" Dillon finally said.

The words fought their way out of Menard's mouth. "McNally, a—well never mind, except that, that he's a native of 3-Freewall. He told me about *Hoxha* vanishing from the battle. They've got a tradition at 3-Freewall about that. They look for rocks."

Dillon turned back to his piloting with a snort of disgust. Albrecht continued to stare at Menard with an expression of mild disbelief. "Rocks?"

"My job is tracing xenics," said Menard earnestly. He had to make this make sense. God had handed him what might be the most important discovery in human history. "One, well, idea about xenics is that they are present among us. Internalism, that's called. One branch of Internalism claims they travel in spaceships, or starships, disguised as rockballs. Asteroids.

"There's anecdotal evidence from the second battle of 3-Freewall that *Enver Hoxha* somehow overtook or was overtaken by a rock that was making its own course corrections, immediately before she vanished. Now you tell me she's here, several hundred light-years from her last known location. Even though there's never been a shred of evidence or rumor of her traveling from 3-Freewall to Halfsummer. At best, that's two dozen c-transitions. There aren't enough dark beacons in alignment to make that many hidden legs to a journey.

"And the clincher... ship disappearances, or

translocations, are one of the traces we've always watched for xenic activity. Here you have the biggest confirmable translocated ship in human history. On top of some other evidence in my bureau that Halfsummer is a focus of xenic activity right now.

"We might be about to prove the existence of xenics, and answer the xenic question, in one move."

Menard sighed. He felt spent.

Albrecht finally filled the long silence that followed. "And here I thought it was insurance fraud."

"Fucking xenics," said Dillon. "Never liked them around."

Menard and Albrecht both stared at him.

#

Golliwog: Halfsummer Solar Space, The Necklace, Shorty's Surprise

It didn't work. He had about twenty seconds to go, and the fog wasn't reacting. Just swirling, shimmering. It knew he was there, it wouldn't touch him.

He needed a counterweight, some thing to swing against or throw away.

Throw away.

Sixteen seconds.

Yee or the angel.

Fourteen seconds.

Who did he owe? What did he owe?

Twelve seconds.

What was he? Who was he?

Ten seconds.

The memory of the priest's sad eyes brought Golliwog to tears.

Eight seconds.

"God damn me," he said, and grabbed the line holding the life bubbles in place.

Six seconds.

He strained his muscles to shift his orientation relative to Dr. Yee and the angel, transferring momentum to the two life bubbles.

Four seconds.

He swung harder.

Two seconds.

He unclipped the line and cast one bubble loose.

And his trajectory shifted. The nano bloomed bright, the probability curves opened up inside Golliwog's head, as he hugged the remaining life bubble close.

"Go with God, Dr. Yee," he whispered.

If someone bothered to pick her up in the minutes of life remaining to her, they might be willing to help. The angel was a made thing, like him. They both stood outside the kind regard of both God and man.

Any sane human would kill it on sight.

And besides, whispered his traitor voice, *she would have cut you open for the secret of c-transition* .

Clutching the angel close, trailed by a blaze of defensive nano, Golliwog headed for the mass hauler. From there he could make a hop to *Jenny's Little Pearl*.

He'd already made his hop away from being human.

Golliwog wept.

#

He was almost five minutes into his ten-minute reserve when he made *Pearl*'s main airlock, the angel once more lashed to his left shoulder. Golliwog could go a long time without breathing, but his skin still respired, and even he needed his next breath. Maybe he had a ten-minute margin once his oxygen ran flat. Sitting in all that carbon dioxide wasn't going to do him much good.

Golliwog studied the access panel. Locked and dark. No wonder his benefactors had slipped him the codelock key.

If he guessed wrong about which ship it was for, he wouldn't have very much time for regrets.

Golliwog slipped the codelock key from the utility bag. The bag itself wasn't vacuum-rated, and the fibers were brittle and crumbling. Much like his life. Golliwog felt a shudder run through his chest, painful against his distressed ribs.

The codelock key slotted into the data port on the access panel. Status lights cycled and the lock opened obediently.

No passwords, no overrides. Maybe he'd live.

He towed the angel into the lock, the two of them crowded—this was a small boarding lock, deliberately undersized to discourage rude strangers in combat armor, he imagined. The outer hatch shut and the chamber began to pressurize. As soon as the ambient air became thick enough for him to hear the hissing of the valves, Golliwog stripped the baggie helmet free.

He promptly gagged, clenching his mouth against the bile that threatened to come up. The stench in the air was unbelievable.

What the hell had happened here?

There was no helping it. He was pretty sure he'd seen the angel breathing vacuum, right before they fought, but in its current state it wasn't likely to be nearly so tough. It needed air, too. He mumbled an apology and popped the seals on the angel's life bubble.

Blood red eyes blinked at him from within. It was curled like a fried eel, tight and small for something so freakishly tall. The angel stared, but did not move.

"Why'd you try to kill us?" Golliwog asked.

Something tickled his carrier, briefly, that same feeling as before, but that was all. The angel blinked once, then continued to stare.

"I think you're dying, friend." Golliwog stared back

a moment longer. "I'm sorry."

He cycled the inner hatch. The stink was worse. As he stepped through, something swept him off his feet with a ear-rending screech, dumping him into too much swampy, fetid water.

On a *spaceship!?* was Golliwog's thought as a great weight pressed against his damaged ribs and huge set of stinking jaws closed on his face.

#

He wasn't unconscious for more than a few seconds, he knew that already. But something was very wrong with his eyes. Golliwog tried to blink, couldn't make it happen. There was a terrible thrashing squeal nearby, then a crack which made the deckplates vibrate beneath his back. Something sloshed through the stench, picked him up gently, and sloshed more, carrying him along.

A few moments later a hatch hissed. The angel—it had to be the angel, Golliwog told himself—carried him through and laid him in a chair.

"My eyes," Golliwog tried to say, and discovered his lips were not working well either.

There were various clicking noises, and the hum of systems coming to life. Something touched his shoulder, and the carrier tingled in his head again. Nano? The angel?

Golliwog concentrated, trying to find sense in the patterns. It was like getting a new implant from the surgeons, the nerves had to learn their way into the interface. He knew that his brain had never been allowed to canalize in the classic juvenile developmental sense—he'd always been able to grow new connections, route around damage or hardened processes.

This had been tickling him for a while.

"Hey…" he mumbled softly.

Now, whispered a voice almost like his traitor

thoughts. But it was from outside.

Golliwog relaxed his own vocal cords and just thought about talking. *Now. Sure.*

Now.

Yes, he thought. *Now. Go. Follow them. It's what you want, right?*

Now. But this time, a different tone.

He heard the angel moving around the bridge, felt a shift in the vibrations as *Jenny's Little Pearl* brought her engines online. It all made sense. *Dmitri Hinton* would follow *Pearl*. So would the priest's ship, whenever it showed.

They would all come to him.

Smiling, Golliwog slept.

#

Albrecht: Halfsummer Solar Space, The Necklace, In transit

"You're both nuts," he said. "Delusional bastards. Xenics this, Black Flag that. Everything's a plot to you people!"

"Does your recent experience suggest otherwise?" Menard asked.

The priest's calm only annoyed Albrecht further, but the man had a point. "I don't know," he said. Control, control. "Some of this is way too convenient. I happen to find the codelock key, you happen to show up knowing about this McNally and his rocks."

"Things happen," said Dillon. "We have about twenty-two hours, by the way. *Hoxha* is very close to crossing over the plane of the ecliptic, so it is not a difficult trip. You may wish to sleep at some point."

"Thanks." Albrecht stared outward at the quiet stars. He couldn't escape properly, he couldn't even get killed properly. Most people drank themselves to death, or got fatally mugged in some dockside corridor. Not him. He had to get involved in revolutions. Or maybe counterrevolutions. "Is someone pushing our buttons?"

"Anything is possible with xenics," said Menard. "If they're here, they've evaded official contact all the centuries of the human experience in space." He added in a satisfied voice: "Until now."

A thought flashed through Albrecht's mind. "Proxies."

"Pardon?"

"Proxies." It made a weird kind of sense. "Every loudmouth in a spaceport bar thinks the Black Flag is a Naval proxy. Provocations to justify the budgets." Dillon snorted loudly but said nothing to this. Albrecht continued, "What if the xenics are using proxies? What if they have their own disagreements? One set knows where *Hoxha* is, doesn't want another set of xenics to have her. Maybe the way to keep her out of their hands is to let the ship become public knowledge once more. Navy would be on that like stink on a recycling tank. So they tip and nudge various of us to find this thing."

"You're in the wrong line of work, my son," said Menard.

Albrecht couldn't decide whether to laugh or shriek at that. "No, I *was* in the right line of work. Far away from all that wheels-within-wheels crap. *Now* I'm in the wrong line of work."

"Xenics are real enough," said Dillon, finally reentering the conversation. "People just don't talk about them. Like a lot of things out here in the Deep Dark. World looks different down a gravity well than it does out here."

"So you seem to have said." Menard's tone was polite, but tense with barely masked fascination. "But you say xenics are real, as in with evidence? We've been searching for centuries."

"From the bottom of your well, Chor Episcopos. Atmospheres bend light. They also bend information. Too much insulation from reality. We won't be a true spacefaring species 'til our masters are born, live, and die in space. That's what the xenics are waiting for."

"Tell me, Ser Dillon," Menard asked quietly. "Have you ever spoken to a xenic?"

"Yes," said Dillon slowly. "And so have you."

"Delusional." Albrecht laughed. "It's all insurance fraud and rebel scams."

Dillon laughed too, his rumble rolling right over Albrecht. "Can be both at the same time. Xenics need money too."

Menard sighed. "If only it were true."

#

Some hours later, Dillon woke Albrecht by the simple expedient of shouting his name until sleep sped away. "You're stacking up a message queue, Ser Albrecht," the pilot said once Albrecht had blinked away enough sleep to respond.

"From who?"

"From *whom*. As it happens, inbound traffic from INS *Dmitri Hinton*, INRS *Novy Petrograd*, and PSS *St. Gaatha*. Oh, and CRS *Swamp Rat*."

Even through the clearing muddle of sleep in his head, Albrecht could spot a new player. "Who the hell is *that?*"

"Fast charter from Halfsummer. Somebody named Gorova on board."

"Oh, joy. They can fight over who gets to arrest my dead body."

"You want to read any of that?"

"Do they say anything besides, 'Stop or I'll shoot'?"

Dillon snorted once more. "Not really. Shorty's

Surprise has informed *Hinton* that some of their crew committed murder and public endangerment while under the parole of *St. Gaatha*'s crew. The Chor Episcopos, they mean." Albrecht glanced at Menard ,who was snoring. "*Hinton* has blamed you, as has *St. Gaatha*. It goes on like that for a while."

"Whoever wanted everything to be public has certainly gotten their wish," Albrecht said. It did make him smile. "Admiralty and the Prime See will be fighting this out for years to come."

"We've got another problem."

"Oh, sure, just like a shuttle, always room for one more. What's that?"

"Your message queue is being forwarded from *Jenny's Little Pearl*. Which is right now on the fastest intercept of all our little friends. *Pearl* is forwarding, but they're not actually talking. I don't know who's flying her."

A plot popped up on Albrecht's panel, shunted over from Dillon's command console. The probability curves were much cruder than what *Pearl* had been able to give him, but Dillon was probably working with a lot less data and certainly working with less sophisticated systems.

Nonetheless, it was a wonder to behold. *Hinton*, *Petrograd*, and *St. Gaatha* were all closing on *Pearl*. Albrecht's recent boat was in turn closing on their rock hopper, with *Swamp Rat* coming up on the inside, much like the dark horse in a yacht race. *Pearl* was going to overhaul their rock hopper before they got to *Hoxha*, or possibly beat them directly to *Hoxha*, by a number of hours if she made the least-time effort—her course was still open to both outcomes.

"Nice," said Albrecht. All his air leaks were coming home for a patch. Then a question occurred to him.

"How did Menard get here ahead of *St. Gaatha*?"

"Rode a message torpedo in ahead of his ship, essentially. Along with his angel."

"Angel? What angel? What the hell *is* an angel?"

"Hot shit Church security. The thing that we let beat the crap out of the Naval Oversight team hunting you. Including a hot-wired bione that I wouldn't care to tangle with. You owe the good Chor Episcopos over there a big one. Or maybe his angel."

Albrecht glanced at the sleeping Menard. The priest didn't look like a killer. Or even a killer's handler. He was a slightly fussy, overfocused Church bureaucrat who seemed to hear God talking in his head. *"Why?* Why was the angel keeping them away from me?"

"I wish we knew," said Dillon.

"I just don't want to go down hard over this."

"Too late, Ser Albrecht. Too late for all of us, I fear."

Albrecht wondered precisely who 'us' was. He hoped like hell it didn't include the inhabitants of Shorty's Surprise. They deserved better than his mistakes.

#

Golliwog: Halfsummer Solar Space, Orbit of NSS Enver Hoxha

Kill, said the angel in his head.

"Me?" asked Golliwog. His voice seemed to be working, a little bit, though his face was a mask of stiff, tight pain. Nothing wrong with his nose. *Pearl* still smelled like wrong end of six kilometers of swampland.

Them.

Them… Albrecht… Menard… the civilians back at Shorty's Surprise. There were so many *thems*. "Why?"

…

He could actually feel the blank surprise. As if he'd

asked, why is there vacuum outside the hull? "Why kill them?"

...

"Is your priest coming?"

Yes.

"Ask him for permission."

...

Golliwog slipped away for a while.

#

The next time he knew where he was, the tone of the ship had changed. Had it been changed the last time? "Are we here?" he asked.

Yes.

"Where you want to kill?"

Yes.

Made thing, he thought. "You can choose not to kill, you know. You can choose. You are better than whoever made you."

...

"Where is here?" He struggled for the name. That itself frightened Golliwog deeply. His memory was by definition perfect. Was this what it meant to be human? To forget? "*Hoxha*," he finally said. "What Yee and Spinks were looking for."

Them.

"Them who?"

Then there was a massive bloom of paranoia and hatred, his head filled with generations of fear and terror of the unknown and the unGodly.

"Xenics," said Golliwog. "Xenics here."

Yes. Somehow, the angel communicated satisfaction.

"Did I tell you that you could choose not to kill? You are more than the sum of what you were made to be." He wondered where Dr. Yee was.

#

Menard: Halfsummer Solar Space, Orbit of NSS Enver Hoxha

"They've picked up a cold corpse," said Dillon. "A Captain Yee. The Navy is very, very pissed. I think *Dmitri Hinton*'s going to come up our asses with guns blazing."

Menard sighed, crossed himself, promised prayers for the dead. Even the unpleasant dead. Both pastoral duty and personal obligation, in this case, though he had serious doubts that Yee had ever acknowledged God. "The last time I saw her she wasn't very healthy, but she was alive." His gut dropped. "And she was under my parole."

"You didn't kill her, Chor Episcopos."

He did not want to weep for the woman, but he had failed her. "I didn't kill Yee by my actions, but I did not protect her either. God forgive me."

"Well, she died to get you here." Dillon rolled the rock hopper along its axis of travel and fired up a set of sun-bright external lights.

There was an enormous hull out there, visible section by section as Dillon's rock hopper moved alongside it. Nothing gave it scale except the number of features crowded onto it. The ship was a mess, too, entire series of hull frames reduced to bent slag, armor and skin peeled away. Parts seemed bent out of true, rendered into shapes that nagged at the eye.

It was staggeringly large, and staggeringly improbable. Menard could barely breathe for the sheer miracle of the thing, feeling once more that shiver of inspiration in his bones, conflicting with the dread lump of failure in his heart. *Oh Lord, You give and You take away. Is this a trial to temper my joy of discovery?* He would celebrate a Divine Liturgy of thanksgiving as soon as possible.

It still wasn't a confirmed xenic contact, but something very strange *had* to have happened to bring that ship here.

"Poolyard wasn't so crazy," said Albrecht in a thoughtful voice. "It is… off. Like it got wrung out and twisted back close to true."

"What does that to a ship?" asked Menard, still marveling at what God had brought him to. *Oh God, please spare me from pride*, he prayed.

"Xenics," said Dillon.

Albrecht glanced at his own console. "Where's *Pearl*?"

Dillon sighed. "Here. Relaying traffic even, but quiet. We're probably lucky she's unarmed."

"Yeah, well. Who's flying her?"

"According to Shorty's Surprise, the Navy bione and the Chor Episcopos's pet angel. They weren't sure about that until Captain Yee turned up dead."

Menard considered that. "They just now told us about her?"

"Much to my irritation," said Dillon. "They had to have known it for the better part of two days. Things are still… unsettled… at home, and will be until we know the truth here."

"Or decide what the truth shall be." Menard asked the question closest to his heart. "And where are the xenics? You say I've spoken to them, but I don't see them here."

"Look for rockballs," said Albrecht.

"Midships," Dillon answered. "Weird mass–energy distortions about the one point eight kilometer mark. That would be 'weird' in the technical sense of the term. We're coming up on it now."

And there something shimmered in the glare of the

rock hopper's lights, a rocky body no different from the asteroids of a thousand solar systems, except that this one was firmly wedged in a hull section of a derelict battleship, limned in a faint red glow.

"The rock ship," Menard said, scarcely daring to breathe. "From 3-Freewall… the *Ulan Ude* recordings." He slumped in his chair, eyes closing, and began to meditate on the welling lump of pride, joy, and fear in his heart.

The xenics were real.

Thank you, God. For showing me this, for allowing me this privilege. Lord Jesus Christ, Son of God, have mercy on me, a sinner.

"Civil war, here we come," said Albrecht.

Dillon squinted, began tapping up new telemetry feeds. "What's that down there, walking on the hull?"

#

Golliwog: Halfsummer Solar Space, Orbit of NSS Enver Hoxha

He woke up once more, seeing double. Well, seeing, but not with his own eyes. Golliwog was pretty sure he didn't have eyes anymore.

Something big and stony rose in front of him. It glowed red, a strange, syrupy red that whispered to him of relativistic shifts and time distortions. He—he?—moved, working patiently at something on a pitted, twisted surface beneath feet that were too far away.

The angel, Golliwog thought.

Greetings.

"What are you doing?"

Choosing.

"Choosing to kill?"

Yes.

"Kill whom? What?"

Them.

The angel looked down at its hands. It carried a power cell, configured for a Mark Seventeen or earlier torpedo. Golliwog knew three ways to make a perfectly good explosive out of one of those. Obviously the angel did, too.

"Xenics again. Why do you hate xenics?"

Wrong.

The hands fitted the power cell next to five others already stacked very close to the red-syrup glow. The angel must have found an unexpended launch rack or magazine nearby.

"You don't hate them?"

No.

"Then why?"

Again, the flood of paranoia, fear, dread. Image of planets burning, ships bursting their air and men into space like seeds lost from an unripe pod.

"They will kill us?"

Selves.

"They will make us kill ourselves?"

Yes. Once more, that air of satisfaction.

Lacking any power but persuasion, and that ineffective at the moment, Golliwog watched the angel work.

#

Albrecht: Halfsummer Solar Space, Orbit of NSS Enver Hoxha

"I'm going out there," Albrecht said. "I started this, I can finish it." He owed Dillon's people that much. Damn it, if he was going to get whacked by the Navy or the Church or some avenging angel, he'd make it mean something.

He'd always wondered what purpose felt like.

Menard unbuckled from his couch. "The angel will kill you before it bothers to look at you. If you're going to go, you have to take me with you."

"No one leaves my boat without my say-so," said Dillon.

"There's a good plan," Albrecht snapped. "I guess we'll just sit here and watch. What, we wait for the heavies to show up, swat us, and duke it out among themselves? I'm going down. I'm going to finish this. Besides, I want to touch that damned battleship, make sure it's real."

"Then we land on the hull and do it together."

"Are you *nuts?*"

Dillon laughed, nasty this time. "It's a *rock* hopper. It's made for close contact with large, uncontrolled masses. Latch those helmets down, boys, I'm going to dump air to get us out fast once we've stopped moving."

#

Albrecht cruised slowly on his hardsuit's jets, armed with the ballspitter. Dillon had reluctantly surrendered his weapon of choice, given that, like Menard, Dillon only wore a skinsuit and had no tolerance for return fire. The belter had brought a damn big rock probe from an outside rack on his hopper's hull, though.

The red-glowing rockship seemed to make its own horizon ahead of Albrecht. The angel—or whatever the hell it was—toiled before the eerie glowing curve, building something brick by brick. As far as Albrecht could tell, it was working in hard vacuum with no protection but its own skin.

For some reason, that was deeply frightening.

Dillon's voice crackled in his earbuds. "Those are power cells. It's setting a trap. Or trying to blow that rock."

"Roger that." He could see *Pearl*, slowly orbiting *Hoxha* at a thousand meters or so of standoff. Was that psychotic bione up there, directing the angel, plotting death?

Albrecht wasn't even sure what he wanted, but blowing everything up wasn't the answer. He knew that. Dillon's people needed to come out okay. And *Hoxha* was history, not the future—he knew that, too. He still figured he had an excellent chance of dying out here, but if so he wanted to die for a good reason. Not just to maintain a botched, century-old cover up. Looking at this weird lightshow, the angel dancing like a pin on the flank of a battleship, he was ready to believe in Menard's damned xenics.

But what did it mean?

The angel turned and looked at him. Space around it shimmered as some sort of radiation field snapped into being, in the shape of... Albrecht had to laugh. The angel had spread its wings.

He raised the ballspitter. Not that high-velocity elastic spheres were going to do much to a vat-grown killer, but then, what use was a stick against a storm? People still screamed at lightning.

This is H. Sap *stepping into space*, Albrecht thought. Biggest thing we've done as a species since we fell out of the trees and decided not to climb back up. But instead of living out here in the Deep Dark, making ourselves a species-home, we return to the branches every night to sleep. Sweet, sweet gravity, that keeps our bones strong and our air stuck down.

Maybe Dillon was right. Maybe the xenics were waiting for this. Or were they hoping for humans to destroy the evidence of First Contact? Factions. Factions within factions. Xenics were no more or less than human, on the evidence.

He wished he'd stayed back in Shorty's Surprise. Those were the most alive people he'd ever seen.

As if answer to that thought, a strange voice crackled

in his earbuds. The heads-up display said it was on *Pearl*'s assigned frequency. "Ca' you he' me?"

"Who is this? The bione?"

"'Go'y'wo'. 'o'y, ca' say i' igh… ight."

The bione sounded like it was in bad shape. Had the newt gotten the drop on the invader? Albrecht had to smile for the poor, stupid thing—like him, trapped far from home, doomed to death by disinterested strangers. Meanwhile, the angel loped toward Albrecht in an eerie, no-gee gait. Menard kept station next to him, crossing the outside of his skinsuit.

Albrecht watched nervously. "Are you controlling it?"

"'is'en. 'oms. Ange' 'lan'ing 'oms."

"Bombs?"

"Yes." That last, strangely clear.

"I know." Albrecht shouldered the ballspitter into firing position. It had a control feed compatible with his hardsuit—both items were civilian gear, after all.

"S'o' i'. Don' kill. Choose."

He had to agree with that sentiment, though he wondered what state the bione was in. The newt had done well, unless the angel had done this. Albrecht cut loose a stream of balls into the angel's red-armored chest. It staggered back as Dillon charged past him with his long blade out, suit jets sputtering.

Albrecht knew an opening when he saw one. He fired his suit jets to cut to his right up the curve of *Hoxha*'s hull, trying to clear the angel and get to the power cells, to unwire them. He was an engineer, by God, this was one thing he could do, while Dillon tangled with red vacuum-breathing death. Maybe more people would live with his help. He spared a thought for the people of Shorty's Surprise.

Someone shrieked. He couldn't tell who, just a voice

crackling in his earbuds while he was too busy to page through the heads-up. Albrecht made it to the power bricks, far too close to that glowing red. He wouldn't put himself in that field for any amount of credits.

Time to focus. Don't look. Release the ballspitter, on a lanyard so it doesn't drift off into cold orbit. Yank the cross-wires. Don't look. How was the angel going to detonate this stuff anyway? Another shriek in his ears. Don't look. Cross-wires gone.

He was slammed down onto the hull, hard. Something scrabbled at his hardsuit for a moment, then pulled clear. He looked up to see the angel toss Dillon into the red field. Dillon slowed, stretched, stopped, impossibly long and molecule-thin, trapped at the boundary.

Time distended, thought Albrecht, his engineer's awareness suddenly working in overdrive. The ultimate crash restraint for a rockship in trouble.

The angel stepped over him, then stopped.

#

Golliwog: Halfsummer Solar Space, Orbit of NSS Enver Hoxha

"Choose," he said. "You are more. I chose life for you. You owe life."

Enemy.

The angel stood over the man who had been trying to disarm the power cells.

"Only by choice!" Golliwog hated the sound of his voice, muddy and broken, but the angel understood him.

Priest.

Menard, the stocky Chor Episcopos, drifted in front of the angel. It turned to face its former master.

"Choose."

The man in the hardsuit lifted slightly from the hull, pulling away from the angel.

"Live."

Life.

The priest reached out slowly and traced the cross on the angel's forehead. The gesture made Golliwog's own forehead ache in a sort of joyous sympathy. Was this why the Godly tattooed their heads? To remind themselves and the rest of the world that they had been touched by the divine? The man in the hardsuit—it must be Albrecht, Golliwog realized, even in the fog of his doubled vision—picked up a power cell and tossed it into the red haze. It stretched and stopped, just as the other man had.

Three more cells followed it, as the priest took the angel's hands and knelt to pray. Golliwog's ruined eyes somehow found more tears for his face.

Then Marines landed. Armored and moving fast as angry vengeance, they shot the angel to a frozen spray of gray, white, and red. Albrecht hurled a fourth cell into the haze. The Marines shot it, exploding to fireworks. The priest gestured frantically, trying to throw himself in front of the guns. Albrecht picked up a fifth cell and charged the Marines, who blew him to spray.

"*Pearl*," said Golliwog through his bloody lips. "Ram them all."

\#

Menard: Halfsummer Solar Space, Orbit of NSS Enver Hoxha

Spinks, the man's name was. Menard didn't much care. This strange, intense officer bore a strong resemblance to the late Captain Yee.

"Chor Episcopos, you must make a choice." The Lieutenant spoke low and fast and hard. They were in a boat deck. The place reeked of sweat and hard-used equipment, and the strange metallic tang of air cycled too many times. Armed and angry Marines were a looming presence all too close by. They had left several of their number trapped in the red field, and more scattered across the hull of the battleship.

Menard had seen what those men would do, but somehow the Lieutenant had bullied and bribed the two of them a short burst of privacy. "I cannot let this go," he told Spinks.

"You know too much. I would not slay a priest, but we must destroy *Enver Hoxha* and every record of her. She is a threat to the peace of the entire Empire. Even the memory of this ship's being here would cause riot. My surgeon can be very selective in the trauma she induces. You need only lose the last day or two of your recollection."

Menard sank to the deck and looked up at Spinks in supplication. This couldn't be why God had led him here, to find and lose everything in the same stroke. "We have been waiting all these millennia for this moment. And you will destroy it? Destroy me? And destroy our hope of knowing the xenics in this lifetime."

"You're an idiot," snarled Spinks. "Xenics have been among us for generations. Proof will come out some day, but not this day. The Empire would tear itself apart in witch hunts and crusades."

"How do *you* know?" Menard asked bitterly.

"Yee was a xenic. Chor Episcopos, I am too."

Menard was suddenly certain he would not be allowed to live out the hour, knowing this much, but he had to ask: "*How?*"

Spinks sighed. "Once we were long and thin and pale, and lived in holes by the banks of rivers. We mimic, at the cellular level. With absolute fidelity. But only... intelligent... predators. All of which were extinct on our world by the time humans came.

"Xenics have been among humans for generations.

We have become human. Humans have become us. It is no different from being Alfazhi, now. Just another racial variant. We breed true with other humans and with each other. We're tougher, heal faster, live longer, but not outside the edges of human norm."

It was eerily possible. And would explain so much. And that poor, doomed Micah Albrecht had thought he had a handle on an insurance scam. Despite himself, Menard followed the trail. At least *he* would know, before the end came to him. "And you run the Navy?"

"Only parts of it." Spinks grinned humorlessly. "Some of us stand outside, some work from within. The outsiders have… more technology, less understanding. They walk through c-transition, fly faster than any humans can. The insiders fight them off, defend the status quo. Your Patriarch is terrified of us. He does not know or care about the difference between our factions. His fear is different. If we can become human, what does that say of your place in creation, your souls?"

"It says…" Menard stopped. Spinks stood before him, panicked, angry, breathing hard. A man with a soul. Right?

Who was human in God's eyes?

Oh, Lord, such a challenge You have set Your followers. How shall we know who is deserving of Your grace?

Menard could have lived a thousand years to meditate and pray upon that question. In that moment, he would have given almost anything for the chance to do so.

Spinks rushed on, with the look of a man battling time. "The Patriarch knows, some of his advisors do. The angels… are xenic hunters. That's who they protect against, at the Prime See. Me and mine."

"You and yours." The Patriarch *knew*. He didn't

doubt those words, not here and now, though it was betrayal of Ekumen Orthodoxy. To know a thing about God's creation, and then deny it... that bordered on sin. But they knew. He could have wept.

Bitterness flooded back into Menard's soul, God suddenly too far away. What was Russe about? Why did the Xenic Bureau exist then, he wondered. To let the hierarchy know when the truth had drawn too near. No wonder they'd sent the angel with him. They'd been afraid Menard might actually stumble onto the truth.

Anger flared into the bitterness. "And that Golliwog?"

"We have... projects. Improvements. Works in progress. Things we've learned."

"Angel killers," said the priest, trying to keep his unworthy emotions out of his tone of voice.

"Killers and much, much more. We're trying to walk through c-transition, too, Chor Episcopos. In sheer self-defense." Spinks glanced back at his restive Marines. "Enough questions. We are out of time. You're either convinced, or you never will be. Choose now."

Menard shook his head, eyes filling with tears. "You offer to take my memory. Such a bargain, my knowledge in exchange for my life. The world is sinful enough without me compounding it with error. Your answer leaves me no closer to God or to the truth, Lieutenant. Shoot me now and have done with it."

Spinks waved the Marines over. "Drop him in the rock with the rest of them. Maybe he'll have another chance someday."

#

Menard tumbled through space, praying. He was headed for the syrupy red glow that had swallowed both Dillon and *Pearl*. Albrecht and the angel were just glittering fog in the vacuum, drifting away from the xenic ship.

He wondered which fate was worse. The little homing rocket the Marines had strapped to his back kept his course true, but Menard didn't even try to fight it.

A snatch of an old hymn crossed his mind, "Oh hear us when we cry to Thee; for those in peril on the sea."

Down he went, into the red, rolling slowly as he fell into whatever time trap had protected the rockship, and the truth, this last century. Would he go to God now? It was an event horizon down there, a sort of imitation black hole. Menard's soul might be trapped in the last second of his life 'til eternity drew to a close.

Even that stirred his imagination. He might see the end of time. God's plan come to fruition. That would be worth delaying his salvation.

In his last moments in this time, Menard saw batteries on *Dmitri Hinton* glow with the ionization of prefiring. Setting the contact trail to their targets along *Hoxha*'s hull. It was like calling shots, though he couldn't imagine how long it would take Spinks to blast this monster into junk. Then he realized it was not *Hoxha* that *Hinton* sought to kill. There was a blaze of energy as missiles from a distant source struck the Naval ship.

St. Gaatha, come calling for her dead angel and her fallen priest.

Civil war had arrived, even without *Hoxha*.

"Too late, McNally," he said as he committed his soul to God. "Watch out for rocks."

That final word was swallowed in the blue deeps of time as fire erupted around Menard in the heavens.

About the Author

Jay Lake has been described as one of the rising stars of the science fiction and fantasy genre. Since first appearing on the scene in late 2001, he has seen over 240 short stories published, along with four novels out, and four more forthcoming over the next few years. His work has received starred reviews in Publisher's Weekly and Booklist, and significant recognition within the science fiction and fantasy field. He has won two of the most prestigious awards in science fiction and been nominated for numerous others.

Lake was born and raised overseas as the son of a United States diplomat. His childhood experiences in Asia, African and Europe have given him a wealth of cultural and geographical detail to draw from when creating exotic settings and strange situations. He has, after all, lived them. His professional career has been in advertising and marketing for the high technology field, which gives Lake a lifetime of exposure to technology issues and trends. Taken together, these go a long way to explaining his choice of writing fields.

Lake is a frequent guest at writing conferences and conventions, where his readings are well attended. He also workshops with newer writers, paying forward all the help and mentoring he has received and continues to benefit from. With his distinctive attire and quirky, improvisational humor, Lake is a familiar figure and a fan favorite all over the West Coast.

He also maintains a blog which has been ranked as

a top 25 science fiction blog. There Lake talks about writing, photography, politics, his experiences as a parent, as well as posting travelogs of his trips to some unlikely destinations, such as a recent outing to a long-abandoned Titan I missile silo. Lake also regularly posts online reprints of his older work, and a biweekly podcast consisting of recorded readings, panels and interviews conducted during his travels.

Today Jay Lake lives in Portland, Oregon, where he works on multiple writing and editing projects. His 2007 book Mainspring received a starred review in Booklist. His 2009 novels include *Mainspring*, *Escapement*, and *Green* from Tor Books, and *Trial of Flowers* and *Madness of Flowers* from Night Shade Books. His short fiction appears regularly in literary and genre markets worldwide. Jay is a winner of the John W. Campbell Award for Best New Writer, and a multiple nominee for the Hugo and World Fantasy Awards. Jay can be reached through his Web site at www.jlake.com.